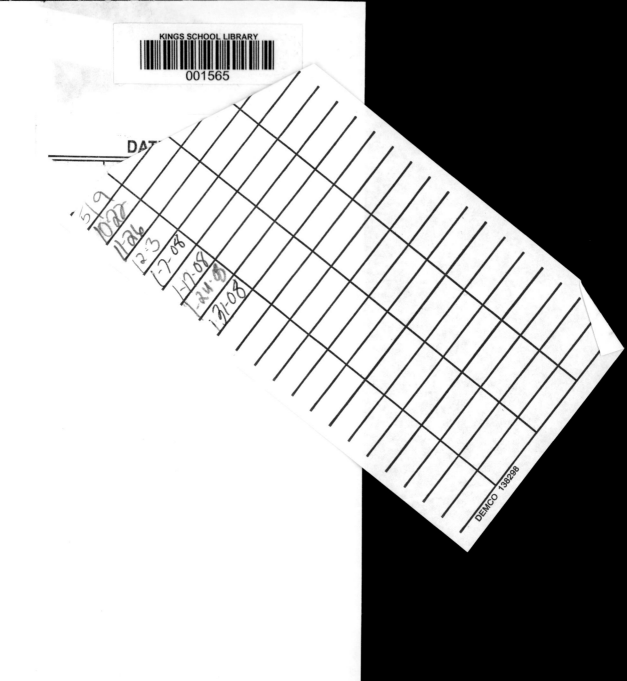

DAT

DEMCO 138298

thunder from the Sea

Joan Hiatt Harlow

ALADDIN PAPERBACKS
New York London Toronto Sydney

This book is a work of fiction. Any references to historical events, real people, or real locales are used fictitiously. Other names, characters, places, and incidents are the product of the author's imagination, and any resemblance to actual events or locales or persons, living or dead, is entirely coincidental.

ALADDIN PAPERBACKS

An imprint of Simon & Schuster Children's Publishing Division

1230 Avenue of the Americas, New York, NY 10020

Copyright © 2004 by Joan Hiatt Harlow

All rights reserved, including the right of reproduction in whole or in part in any form.

ALADDIN PAPERBACKS and colophon are registered trademarks of Simon & Schuster, Inc.

Also available in a McElderry Books for Young Readers hardcover edition.

Designed by Sammy Yuen Jr.

Map by Kristan Jean Harlow

The text of this book was set in LombaBook.

Manufactured in the United States of America

First Aladdin Paperbacks edition June 2005

10 9 8 7 6

The Library of Congress has cataloged the hardcover edition as follows:

Harlow, Joan Hiatt

Thunder from the sea / Joan Hiatt Harlow.—1st ed.

p. cm.

Summary: Just when his dreams of being part of a family and having a dog seem to be coming true, Tom wonders if trouble with neighbors on his new island home and the impending birth of a new baby will change everything. Set in Newfoundland in 1929.

ISBN 0-689-86403-5 (hc.)

[1. Orphans—Fiction. 2. Dogs—Fiction. 3. Family life—Newfoundland and Labrador—Fiction. 4. Newfoundland and Labrador—Fiction.] I. Title.

PZ7.H22666Th 2004

[Fic]—dc21

2003010687

ISBN 0-689-86404-3 (pbk.)

To Jordan, Madison, and Jacie,
with love and hugs . . . and a bit of jannie talk from
Noanie

NOWDEESTREEMAIDSIS'BOUTDEELOVEEYEST'NBYFAR
DEEPRETTIEST'NBRIGHTESTSWEETARTSI'VEEVER
SEENINALLMEBORNDAYS!
AN'IJUSTLOVES'EMTOPIECES!

thunder
from
the Sea

contents

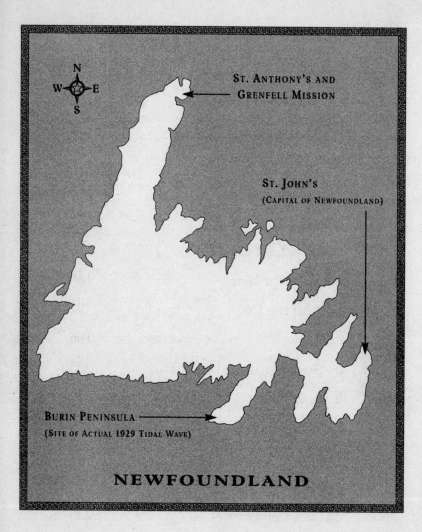

ST. ANTHONY'S AND
GRENFELL MISSION

ST. JOHN'S
(CAPITAL OF NEWFOUNDLAND)

BURIN PENINSULA
(SITE OF ACTUAL 1929 TIDAL WAVE)

NEWFOUNDLAND

tom Campbell held on to the rail as the *Constance* rose and fell in the giant swells of the ocean. Tom's stomach rolled along with the tossing of the waves. *A fine fisherman I'll be if I get seasick like this,* he told himself. *What will Mr. Murray think?* The steamer continued churning through the heavy surf. Tom bent over the side of the ship and yucked up his lunch into the ocean.

He looked over his shoulder, hoping Mr. Murray hadn't seen him. After all, the man was taking a big chance on thirteen-year-old Tom by bringing him into his home to live and onto his boat to work.

He let the roaring wind blow in his face, breathing deeply and praying that they'd soon be at his new home. For the past ten years, home had been the orphanage at the Grenfell Mission in St. Anthony on the Northern Peninsula. It was the only home Tom could remember.

He was born in Labrador and sometimes when he smelled pine trees or the scent of fish cooking on an open fire, a faint memory would present itself—a fleeting recollection of voices and shadowy faces. He remembered being feverish and his mother rocking him and crooning a lullaby in cheek music—the music Newfoundlanders made up and sang to themselves or their children. *Falalalee. Falalaloo.* The memory was faint and hazy, like a dream.

Both his parents became ill when he was three years old and they were all taken on the hospital ship to the mission. When his parents died, Tom stayed on at Grenfell. He lived in the school and learned to farm potatoes, beets, and turnips for the long winters. The good people there were kind, but not a true family.

Now it was 1929 and at last he'd be living in a real home with fisherman Enoch Murray and his wife, Fiona. Mr. Murray seemed nice enough, but quiet and shy, as if he didn't know what to say to

Tom. Tom wasn't a bit sure what to say to *him*, either.

He felt another surge of nausea and he leaned over the rail again, upchucking what was left in his belly. He'd never be a fisherman! Right now he positively *hated* the sea!

"Are you feelin' squawmish, lad?" Mr. Murray was suddenly next to him. "You look green in the gills."

"Aye, I'm a bit sick to the stomach, sir," Tom answered.

"It's shockin' rough today. Could be an August gale blowin' up from the northeast."

"I don't usually get seasick, Mr. Murray."

"Call me Enoch. We'll both feel more t'ease usin' first names." Enoch squinted at the horizon. "We should be home by tomorrow mornin'. Maybe it'll calm down tonight and you can get some sleep. I ordered a cabin for the night. I didn't have the money for two, but I think you're the one who needs it most." He handed Tom a key with the number 21 on it. "It's down that way." He pointed toward the back of the boat.

"Thank you . . . Enoch," Tom said. "I promise I won't always be like this."

Enoch nodded, but didn't smile. Was he regretting that he'd brought Tom back to live with him to help him with his fishing business? Tom felt almost too sick to care.

But he truly *did* care. He'd often wished for a real family in a real house. And now that it finally might be happening, he didn't want to ruin everything.

He wondered if the Murrays had a dog—one that he could run and play with, one that would be his friend. That would make everything perfect.

Tom made his way down to the cabin, hanging on to the rail as the boat continued lurching. Once inside cabin 21, he reached into his pocket and pulled out the one treasure he owned—his grandfather's pocket watch. He opened it. Five o'clock. It was too early to go to bed but he was sick and he just wanted to sleep.

Tom clicked the watch shut. His fingers traced the Celtic knot that was engraved on the cover. He tucked the watch under the pillow, just as he always did, then sank onto the cot, hearing the comforting muffled *ticktock, ticktock*, like a heartbeat.

The *Constance* continued rocking—rocking—but now he was in his mother's arms and she was singing the lullaby. *Falalalee. Falalaloo.*

When Tom awoke he looked out the porthole. The waves had subsided and the August sun sparkled on the water. He had slept here all night! Mr. Murray . . . Enoch . . . didn't have his turn to use the cabin! Tom got up, washed his face in the small sink, put his watch back in his pocket, then went looking for Enoch. He found him standing on the deck.

"Sleep well?" Enoch asked.

"Yes, sir. I never woke once. I'm sorry. I didn't mean to hog the stateroom."

"It's all right, lad." Enoch pointed to the cliffs. "We'll be home soon. Just beyond there is a narrow harbor that will take us to Back o' the Moon Island. It's a small island with several families that's just opposite Chance-Along, the nearest town."

"How do you get to Chance-Along?"

"By wagon and boat. There's a rickety bridge at the end of the island. Sometimes it gets washed out in storms."

"You must have a horse, then?"

"My neighbor, Amos Bosworth, and I bought one together. You'll meet Amos. He's a crousty rogue, but not bad once you get to know him." Enoch looked Tom up and down. "He has a son your age named Bert—a right laddio like his pa. Gets in trouble a lot. And they have a girl, too. Nancy. And then there are the Rideouts. They've got a boy, Eddie, and a wee girl, Rowena. Ken's a fisherman like me, and Margaret, his wife, is the island's granny—you know, a neighborhood nurse that delivers babies and takes care of sick folk."

At the big hospital mission where Tom had lived, he had heard the doctors there talk about "grannies" who treated illnesses with herbs and delivered babies in the outports. He'd also heard about the "charmers" who used magic to heal. Tom also knew stories about charmers who, just by holding their thumbs over an aching tooth, could ease the pain, or stop a nosebleed by tying a green satin ribbon around your neck. The doctors at the mission warned folks about charmers, but they respected the grannies who helped sick people with herbal medicine and common sense.

"It'll be right nice to meet new friends," Tom said. "Enoch, do you have a dog?"

"Nope. No dog."

Tom sighed. He figured a dog was just too much to hope for. He gazed out at the shoreline, which was closer now.

"That's Chance-Along." Enoch pointed to a white church spire and houses that clustered together on the side of the rocky coast. "It's a right modern town. They've even got electricity." He patted Tom's arm. "You'll be on solid ground soon, my boy."

"I'll feel better then," Tom said. "I don't usually yuck like I did yesterday."

"It was pretty rough on the sea yesterday," Enoch said.

As the steamer moved toward shore, Tom could see dozens of fishing boats tied up against the wharves. All along the waterfront, thousands of codfish were drying in the sun on the tall flakes—

stages built of tree limbs and branches. *Chance-Along is a busy town,* he thought.

The steamer glided neatly to the dock. As men jumped off and tied the ship to the wharf with huge ropes, Enoch and Tom gathered their bags and stood in line on the gangplank. "There's Fiona!" Enoch pointed to a blond woman waving from a horse-drawn wagon up by the dirt road. She motioned to them and called, "Hello!" as they hurried up the boardwalk to the road.

A dark-haired boy popped up suddenly from the back of the wagon. "I wonder why Fiona brought Bert Bosworth along," Enoch said, frowning.

Bert got out of the wagon. He stood with his hands on his hips and his navy blue eyes narrowed, as if he were sizing Tom up.

Enoch dumped their bags into the back of the wagon, and then introduced Tom to Bert. "You be civil to him," Enoch cautioned Bert.

"'Course I will." Bert grinned at Tom.

"Come meet Fiona," Enoch said, walking to the front of the wagon. As Tom turned to follow him, Bert stuck out his foot, tripping Tom, who fell to his knees. Tom got up and dusted off his pants and his hands without a glance at the boy, who stood by, laughing. Tom was furious and ready to pummel him, but knew this wasn't the time to take on Bert Bosworth.

"Hello, Tom." Fiona was sitting in the driver's seat. She held out her hand. "I'm glad you've come to live with us."

She was pretty, and when she smiled, little crow's-feet appeared at the corners of her gray eyes. She looked about the same age as Enoch—around forty, he reckoned—but Enoch had dark hair, and eyes that were an unusual golden color.

"Let's go home," Fiona urged, moving over for Enoch to take the reins. "I can't wait to show you your room." She patted the seat next to her. "Tom, you sit up here with us." She turned to the other boy. "Get in the back, Bert."

Bert grumbled, but climbed into the rear of the wagon. The horse snorted and shook his head, as if ready to move on.

"What's the horse's name?" Tom asked as he climbed aboard. Enoch clicked the reins and the horse trudged down the road.

"Prince." Fiona laughed. "Pretty ordinary

name, eh? Practically every horse around here is named Prince."

"I had the right to name him, 'cause he's half ours!" Bert said from the back.

"I would have named him Star," Fiona whispered to Tom. "He has a pretty star on his forehead."

"Star is a nice name," Tom agreed.

They moved down a hill and crossed a rickety bridge. A sign read, "Back o' the Moon Island." On the other side of the bridge stood a church that needed paint. The grounds around the building were overrun with weeds. "We ain't had a preacher in Back o' the Moon for years. Anyone who wants to go to church needs to go to Chance-Along," Enoch explained.

"We read our Bible every Saturday night," Fiona explained. "What more do we need than that?"

"I love the Bible stories," Tom told her. "Especially the one about Elijah and the Baals."

"You like to read, then?"

"Aye, I love to read. It's like goin' somewhere else."

Fiona took a long look at Tom. "My, you're a right smart lad!"

Tom flushed and changed the subject. "Enoch says you don't have a dog."

"No, but a good workin' dog is just what we need." Fiona nudged Enoch. "Eh?"

"Maybe someday," Enoch answered.

Bert spoke up behind them. "I wants a dog. We needs one more than you do! We got a bigger house and . . ."

Fiona shook her head at Bert and winked at Tom.

"How comes you brought Bert?" Enoch muttered under his breath.

"He nagged his mother until she finally said yes," Fiona answered softly.

"Why didn't *you* say no?" Enoch asked.

"I don't dare say no to a Bosworth!" Fiona whispered.

Tom decided that he would stay away from the Bosworth family. He didn't want trouble, and Bert was trouble for sure.

Back o' the Moon was a small island separated from the mainland by a narrow harbor called Rumble Reach. "It's called Rumble Reach because of the sound the tides make when they come in and fill the harbor," Fiona explained to Tom. "We often cross over to the mainland by boat, as it's more direct." She pointed to a white house that looked across the water from a rocky cliff. "That's our place," she told Tom. "There's a shed out back where we keep chickens."

"And there's my house. The big green one." Bert gestured to a boxy dwelling near the shore, close to the flakes and the docks. "And we have a barn over in the back meadow. We keep Prince there so's he can graze in the pasture." He pointed to a square yellow house near the top of the hill.

"Eddie Rideout lives in that house. He's my best chum."

The wagon rounded a curve and headed up a hill to the white house. Enoch stopped at the gate and tied Prince to the fence. Inside the fence was a garden of larkspur and tiger lilies.

Tom climbed out and was about to reach for his carpetbag that carried the few belongings he brought with him, when Bert grabbed it. "I'll take it in," he offered. Tom shrugged but watched Bert uneasily. He hoped the Bosworth boy wouldn't open the latch and let everything fall out. But Bert lugged the satchel through the open door and into the living room where he set it on the rug.

"Thank you, Bert," Fiona said. "You can go on home now and tell your mother you were right helpful. Tom needs some time to get acquainted with things."

Tom's small room faced the meadow and the ocean to the east. It was a clean room with green and white striped wallpaper and shiny cream-colored woodwork. White curtains shifted in the breeze from the open window and a bright quilt covered the bed. The floor was linoleum that looked like hardwood. Tom could tell that the Murrays had recently spruced up the room, as it smelled faintly of fresh paint.

"It's a right nice room," Tom said to Enoch and Fiona who stood by the door. "Thank you."

"We hope you'll be happy here," Fiona said.

They left him to put away his clothes and clean up. Tom folded the quilt and put it on the chair, then lay on the crisp sheets. The soft flutter of the curtains sounded like music and he wished he could sleep for a while. But no! He must get downstairs to see what work Enoch expected of him. He didn't want to seem like an idle slinger. He straightened the bed and then headed down to the kitchen.

Fiona had tea simmering on the black wood-stove. "I've opened the doors and windows to let the breeze in," she said. "The stove makes the house very hot."

"It's a fine house," Tom said, looking around. "Where's Enoch?"

"Down on the beach." Fiona motioned to the table, then poured tea into a beaker. "Sit down,

Tom. It'll be pleasant to have three at the table at last." She set the tea in front of Tom. "We've always wanted children," she said, "but the Lord felt differently, it seems. So we're glad to share our home with a good boy like you. The people at the mission said you were hardworking and well mannered and that you had a good heart." She patted Tom's hand. "Those are praiseworthy words, Tom."

Tom smiled at Fiona. But he didn't know what to say, so he sipped his tea and looked away.

After tea and molasses buns, Fiona led Tom out to the fenced-in yard. She opened the gate, and the chickens cackled and chattered around them. A red rooster chased Tom, clucking and nipping at his trousers. Fiona shooed the bird away. "That's Rufus!" she said. "Once he knows you're part of our family, he'll leave you alone."

Part of the family? Did he dare to hope he'd be part of the family?

"I hope he didn't hurt you." Fiona brushed off Tom's trousers. "Rufus is a sassy bird. You won't need to get the eggs for me until he gets to know you better." She uncovered an egg from one of the nesting places and put it in her apron pocket. She pointed at a lean-to shack. "Over there's the wood shed. That's where we keep firewood and root vegetables."

After lunch Enoch took Tom down to the waterfront where he was repairing a small punt. The boat was turned upside down and the bottom had been scraped. Enoch showed Tom how to caulk the seams by rolling hemp oakum until it was a thread, and then stuffing it into the cracks.

"As soon as that's done, we'll put tar on it," Enoch said. "This old tub'll be fine, once it's watertight, see. When we're sure it's seaworthy, you can have it for your own."

"My own boat?" Tom gasped.

"Why sure, my boy. You're goin' to be a fisherman. With a little punt like this you can fish with hand lines or jiggers, or nets, for that matter. A fisherman needs a boat." Enoch looked thoughtful. "Maybe we'll paint it a bright color so it'll stand out on the water, see."

"Bright red would be a real standout," Tom suggested.

"Red, eh?" Enoch smiled and clamped Tom on

the shoulder. "Let's see what kind of a job you can do on this. I'm goin' down to the boat. Got to fill her up with gas for tomorrow." Enoch left and Tom went immediately to work.

Tom couldn't believe his good fortune. His own little punt! Maybe he would be a good fisherman after all! He was so busy with the caulking he was startled when he saw Bert and another boy standing beside him.

"This here's my chum Eddie," Bert said. Eddie nodded and grinned.

"Why are you botherin' with that old tub?" Bert asked.

"It'll sink soon as it hits the water," Eddie said.

Tom kept on working and didn't answer.

Bert egged him on. "Don't you know how to talk?"

"What are you smouchin' around me for?" Tom asked without looking up.

"I ain't smouchin'."

"You are so. You're prowlin' around tryin' to make trouble!"

"I'm tryin' to be *friendly*"—Bert's voice rose— "since you're goin' to be livin' here."

"Sure don't sound friendly to me," Tom said. "Sounds more like pickin' a fight. And what's the idea of trippin' me in town today with your big clumsy spaug?"

"My spaug got in the way, that's all," Bert answered.

A girl came out from under the tall spindly flakes and headed toward them. She had a little redheaded girl in tow, who seemed about five years old.

"Go on home, Nancy," Bert yelled.

"Go home yourself!" the older girl shouted back and came alongside the punt. "Are you Tom Campbell who's come to live with the Murrays?" she asked. "I'm Nancy, Bert's sister."

Tom immediately saw the resemblance. She had the same raven-colored hair and vibrant blue eyes. *Is she as nasty-mouthed as her brother?* he wondered. "Yes, I'm Tom Campbell."

The little girl tugged at Nancy's hand. "Stop pullin' me," Nancy whispered. "This here's Rowena Rideout, Eddie's sister. I take care of her almost every day. Her ma's the granny here on Back o' the Moon."

Bert interrupted his sister. "Say, Tom. I heard you got sick on the boat yesterday. You better not yuck all over me tomorrow!"

Tom wondered how Bert heard he'd been sick. Did Enoch complain to the Bosworths? He hoped not. But how else could Bert have known? "What am I doin' with you tomorrow?" Tom asked.

"We're goin' out to fish," Bert answered. "My pa and me, with you and Enoch."

"Are you comin' too?" Tom asked Eddie.

"Naw, the boat's only big enough for a crew of four," Eddie said.

Tom turned back to his work. "Then I'll see you tomorrow," he said, hoping Bert would take the hint and go away.

Instead, Bert and Eddie sat on a rock and watched Tom caulk the punt while Nancy and Rowena stood nearby.

"I heared you're an orphan," said Bert.

"Hush!" Nancy warned her brother.

The Murrays must have told the Bosworths all about him. "Yes, my folks died a long time ago."

"How long did you live in the orphanage?" Eddie asked.

"Most of my life. It's not just an orphanage. It's a hospital and school and—"

"That's not what I heared," said Bert.

"What would you know about it?" Tom asked.

"A school's where you learn to read and write and do numbers," said Bert.

"That's right. I learned to read and write and do numbers there," said Tom.

"You can read?" Nancy's eyes were huge.

"Of course I can read! Can't you?" Tom answered.

There was a long moment before anyone spoke. Eddie was watching Bert closely. Then Bert said, "Sure I can read."

"You cannot!" Nancy said.

"I can so," Bert yelled at her.

"He can read and write his name, but that's all," Nancy said to Tom.

"You shut up, Nan. *You're* the one who can't read." Bert spit on his finger and wrote on a boulder. The letters disappeared quickly in the sun, but Tom knew he had written his first name.

"See?" Eddie said. "Bert *can* read and write."

"Write another word," said Nancy.

"I'll write the word *fish*," said Bert with a mean look at his sister. He spit on his finger again. COD.

Tom bent over laughing. "That's not *fish*!" he finally managed to say. "That's *cod*!"

"Well, a cod's a fish, ain't it?" Bert roared, his face red with anger. He stood up, then raced away toward his house down the shore.

"Hey!" Eddie called, running after him. "Wait for me!"

Nancy was still sitting on the rock. "I wants to learn to read real bad. Don't suppose you could teach me sometime, do ya?"

"Maybe," Tom answered. "Isn't there a school in Chance-Along?"

"Yeah, but it's too far to go every day." Nancy chased after Rowena, who was roaming under the flakes, then pulled her back to a boulder and wagged her finger. "You'll get lost someday if you wander off like that." She turned to Tom. "Come on, Tom. We could come over by 'n' by, and you could show me—"

"And me, too," Rowena interrupted.

"I don't know, Nancy. Why don't your folks teach you?"

She looked down at her feet. "Pa's too busy. And Ma can't read, although she pretends she can." She reached over and grabbed Tom's sleeve. "Promise you won't tell *anyone* that my ma can't read. And don't tell *anyone* that you're goin' to teach me. I want to surprise Ma. And Bert would just make fun of me, see?"

"I didn't say I'd—"

"Let me know when we can start," Nancy interrupted, getting up to leave. "When I'm older, if I can read, I can get a real job somewhere— maybe even in St. John's." Nancy took Rowena's hand and headed down the shore. "Don't forget!"

Tom went back to pounding the hemp oakum into the cracks with angry wallops. How did he get himself into this? He'd been at Back o' the Moon one day and already he had to be a fisher- man and a teacher as well! Even worse—Bert was just beggin' for a fight!

I'm biting off more than I can chew with those Bosworths, he thought.

that evening at supper, Tom could tell Fiona had made this first meal together a special event. The table was covered with a beautiful tablecloth. At a closer look Tom could see that it had been made from flour sacks and embroidered with daisies. Fiona lit candles in brass candlesticks. "The kerosene lanterns stink, but these candles smell right nice. They're made from real expensive beeswax, and we don't use them much."

"Havin' Tom livin' with us *is* a big occasion," Enoch said.

Fiona filled dinner plates with pot roast, carrots, and mashed potatoes and placed them on the table.

After saying grace, Enoch said, "We'll be gettin' up at dawn to go fishin'."

"Bert said he and his pa would be comin' with us," Tom said.

"Yes, we often go together," Enoch told him. "Amos is a snapper—a skilled fisherman—even though he's somewhat of a bullamarue."

"Bert's a bullamarue too," said Tom. "He's a show-off and a bully!"

"He's just tryin' you out."

"Well, I'll show him I'm not goin' to be bullied," Tom stated.

"Ah, good for you!" Fiona applauded. "He needs someone to stand up to him. And I think he'll back down once he realizes he can't torment you."

Enoch told Tom how his parents had built the house they were living in, and how his father had bought a boat with a real gasoline engine before he died. "He left me a good tight fishin' boat *and* a gas engine. Not many fishermen in these parts have their own engine," Enoch said proudly.

"We're very lucky to have that boat," said Fiona. "Don't know how we'd manage without it."

"Amos pitches in for expenses and gasoline, and we work together most of the time."

. . .

After a bedtime snack of tea and biscuits with blackberry jam, Tom said good night and went up to bed. He looked out his window and felt a twinge of sadness as he saw the northern lights shifting like windblown red and green curtains across the sky. He suddenly remembered his mother showing him these "merry dancers" when they lived on the Labrador.

Tom undressed and placed his watch under the pillow. The cool sheets smelled of fresh air, sunshine, and balsam. He could hear Fiona singing cheek music as she tidied up the kitchen. "Tooraloora Lorra Lou. Dally wally wooley moo."

Tom felt homesick for the mission. He knew everyone there and what his place was. He recalled Georgie, his best friend. "We'll never have a ma and pa," Georgie would say. "We're too old. We're not babies. All anyone would want from us is to work us to death."

Was Georgie right? Was that all Enoch and his wife wanted from him? Another pair of hands to help around the fishing flakes and wharves? He didn't mind working, but he'd hoped for more than a house and food. Still, Fiona and Enoch had been kind—fixing up the room for him and making him feel welcome.

Tom was drifting off when heard his name spoken from the parlor. He sat up and strained to listen. Enoch and Fiona were talking about *him*.

"I love havin' Tom here," Fiona was saying. "He fills up an empty spot in our home."

"I'm wonderin', though, how he'll be as a fisherman," Enoch said. "He was right sick when we were comin' home on board the *Constance*."

"Stop and think, Enoch," Fiona scolded. "He's leavin' the only home he's ever known to come to this outlandish place to live with strangers. That's enough to make anyone nervous and sick. Besides, it was rough. I'd be chuckin' up my stomach out there myself."

"I know," Enoch admitted. "I've felt those waves in my gut many a time. Still, Tom's a scraggy boy, not too strong. Not like Bert."

"If he were our own, we couldn't choose his build. He could be short and small like my father—who was a strong fisherman and captain, I might add, despite his size." There was a pause, and then Fiona went on. "Tom's a good lookin' boy. In fact, he's a bit like you with those sun-bleached streaks in his coffee-colored hair."

"Tom's a good worker," Enoch went on. "He had that punt completely caulked in no time today."

"I hope he'll feel at home here," Fiona said.

"I just wish he'd open up to us more."

"Be patient, m' dear. He's only been here one day!" Fiona replied.

Their voices became muted and Tom wondered what more they might be saying. Maybe it was just as well that he couldn't hear them. He lay back on the pillow. For so many years he had prayed for a family. Now, would he lose this one because he was too scraggy or too quiet?

Still, Enoch and Fiona had written to the mission for a boy to live with them. They wanted a lad who was good-hearted and the folks at the mission thought of Tom right away. They sent letters and pictures to the Murrays. That was how Fiona and Enoch chose Tom to come live with them.

He prayed silently, as he used to in his cot up north. *Dear Father in Heaven, please don't let me disappoint this family.* As he fell asleep he could hear the rumbling of the incoming tide—the sound of gurgling waves and deep water—and the tick-tick-ticking of his grandfather's watch.

It was still dark when Fiona, carrying an oil lamp, peeked in his room the next morning. "Time to get up, Tom. Breakfast is ready. Put on warm clothes. It can be right cold and stormy on the sea, even in August." She started to the stairs and came back. "Tom, I sure hopes you don't think I'm bein' bossy."

"No. Thanks for remindin' me." Tom dressed in his warm briggs with the leather patches on the knees, his rubber boots, and flannel shirt. He put his fisherman's knit sweater and hat in his nunny-bag.

"Enoch's already down on the wharves," Fiona told him as she placed porridge, tea, and biscuits on the table.

Tom gobbled up his breakfast quickly for fear of keeping Enoch waiting. Then Fiona handed him a paper bag. "Here's your lunch, Tom. I don't think you'll get sick today. It's calm out there right now. You should have a good fishin' day."

Tom went to the door. "See you tonight, Fiona," he said. He sure didn't want her to know that he hadn't been fishing often, although while he was at the mission he had learned how to clean and dry fish and mend nets.

Enoch, Bert, and another man, whom Tom realized must be Amos, were packing the gear on a gray skiff. "Here he is!" Bert yelled when he saw Tom.

Tom jumped on board. No one seemed to notice or care that he was late.

"This here's my pa," Bert said, jerking his thumb toward the robust, red-faced man who was putting oil into the engine through a funnel. He looked up and nodded at Tom.

Enoch and Bert were untangling nets. "Can I help?" Tom asked Enoch.

"We got 'em straightened out," Enoch said. He climbed onto the wharf and untied the bow line. "Start 'er up, Amos," he called to Bert's father. The engine coughed a few times, then rattled and stopped. Amos tried again, and this time the engine started.

"I'll do the stern line," Tom offered. He had

hardly finished untying the knots when Amos put the boat's gear into reverse and began backing into the harbor. Then Amos navigated around the tall white-and-red markers that indicated shoal water. Soon they were heading east.

Bert pointed beyond the narrows and the scarlet sunrise. "Red in the mornin', sailors take warnin'," he recited.

"Yep, could be a storm today," Amos yelled.

The waves began to pick up as they passed through the narrows. Hundreds of black-and-white puffins were nesting on the rocky cliffs of Eastern Head. Gulls dove around them looking for fish. "There's some seals brewin'," Enoch said, pointing to a reef where playful dotards rolled about and splashed their flippers. As the ocean spray tingled on his face, Tom had the same sense of freedom and excitement as the seals. In the distance, two giant icebergs glistened like blue jewels in the sun.

They spent the morning with nets and grapples, and by noon they had a decent catch in the hold. Bert hadn't caused Tom any trouble so far. They pulled in the nets and settled down to eat their lunch. Fiona had made bologna and cheese sandwiches, and Tom felt so well that he ate every bite.

"Great cod! Take a look at that venomous sky," Enoch said, pointing to black clouds that seemed to have suddenly gathered overhead. "There's a shockin' big squall headin' this way!"

Tom watched nervously as a line of black sea moved toward them. Heavy swells began to lift and drop their boat. White surf broke over the bow, splashing around their feet. Enoch began bailing water with the dory piggin. "Got to get the water out. We could swamp in these waves!" Tom found a pan and helped Enoch bail.

Hailstones the size of peas spattered the deck. Lightning streaked across the sky, followed by claps of thunder.

Amos started the motor and turned the boat toward shore. Enoch tossed rolls of canvas to Tom and Bert, who pulled the tarps over themselves. The hail soon stopped, but rain was pouring down in sheets. Enoch continued bailing and Tom, the canvas over his head, kept filling, then emptying his pan overboard as well.

As Tom peered from under the tarp he saw

something bobbing in the fearsome swells, something black. A seal? He squinted and called out to Amos. "There's somethin' in the water off the starboard side!"

Amos turned the wheel to the left, while Tom and Enoch scanned the surging waters in front of them.

"I see it!" Tom yelled. "Go slow!"

Amos cut the engine down while trying to keep the boat on an even keel. "What is it?"

Bert came out from under the tarp. "Why are we stoppin'?"

"Probably just a porpoise or a pothead whale," Enoch said. "Anyway, it's gone."

"No, there it is," Tom shouted. "It's a dog!"

"Nonsense," Amos said with a snort. "How could a dog be out here in the middle of the sea?"

Tom, who hadn't taken his eyes off the water, could now see a slick black head, with shining eyes aimed directly at him. The dog's huge paws paddled madly in the wild surf.

"It *is* a dog. We've got to save him!" Tom stood up untangling his feet from the tarp. "Come on!

Help me!" He reached over and slapped the side of the boat. "Here, boy. Here!"

Enoch yelled to Amos. "We've got to pull 'im on board broadside."

Amos cut the gas down to idling. "It's too dangerous! We could swamp!"

"We can't even see in this rain," Bert yelled. "Let him go! He ain't worth it!"

"Come on, Tom. You too, Bert!" Enoch pulled a net without grapples out from under the bow. "We'll try netting him."

Tom and Enoch each took a side of the net. Muttering, Bert stayed as far from the starboard side as he could. "I'm not riskin' my life for a dumb dog!"

As the dog paddled to the side of the boat, Enoch was just able to cast the net under him. The dog's legs tangled in the net and he struggled to free them. "Get over here, Bert!" Enoch ordered. Grumbling, Bert obeyed, and the trio hoisted the net up onto the deck. The boat tipped perilously as the sopping dog was pulled aboard and water slipped over the gunwales. As soon as the dog was safely on board, Amos pushed the gas lever, turned more to port, and the skiff leveled.

"Where in Sam Hill did that dog come from?" Amos yelled. "There ain't no boat anywheres around that I can see."

"He's 'bout scared to death," Tom said, untangling the dog's paws from the web of hemp ropes. "Poor feller," he whispered. "Where'd you come from, eh?" The dog shook himself, spraying the group that crowded around him; then he whimpered and shivered as another clap of thunder rumbled.

"Looks like we got us a dog," Bert yelled to his father.

"Looks like it," Amos said.

Tom buried his face against the dog's wet fur. This was the beautiful Newfoundland dog he'd dreamed about, and now that he was really here, Tom didn't want to give him up, especially not to Bert.

As if reading Tom's thoughts, Enoch spoke up decisively. "Since Tom is the one who found him, he'll take care of him—until we find the owner, that is."

Bert mumbled something to his father, but

Amos was too engrossed in heading the boat through the rain and waves to hear him.

Tom looked at Enoch gratefully, then wrapped the tarp around the dog and himself. He held his arms around the trembling animal and whispered cheek music into his ears while the skiff made its way to Back o' the Moon Island.

ƒiona, in an oilskin raincoat, was waiting as
they pulled into the wharf and tied up the
boat. "I was worried. Such a wild storm!" Her
eyes fell upon the dog who peered out from
under the tarp. "Where on earth did *that* come
from?"

"Out on the sea," Enoch said, climbing onto
the dock. "Looks like we've got a guest."

"We'll keep the dog, Enoch," Amos argued.
"We need him more than you."

"I told you," Enoch said evenly, "Tom will tend
to the dog. He's the one who rescued him, see? If
the owner isn't found, the dog will be his."

"But I want him, Pa," Bert said, tugging his
father's arm. "He's a real Newfoundland."

Tom crouched silently, clinging to the shivering

dog, and watched the anger rising in Amos's eyes.

"Pa, don't let them take the dog," Bert whined.

"Listen here, Enoch," Amos's voice rose. "We need that dog!"

"Let's not fight over a dog, Amos," Enoch said calmly. "Tom's never had a dog, and this will be a right good experience for him. Bert can come and visit Tom and the dog whenever he wants."

"All right," Amos agreed sullenly, "for now." He climbed from the boat onto the dock.

"Aw, Pa!" Bert pulled himself onto the wharf, glaring at Tom all the while.

"You've got a nice putt of fish in that boat!" Fiona exclaimed, peering into the hold. "Amos, Bert, come up to our house and have a cup of tea to warm up," Fiona invited. "We'll clean and salt the fish later."

"No, we're goin' home." Amos stomped off with Bert at his heels.

Fiona sighed. "Oh, dear. Amos is right mad."

"He'll get over it," Enoch assured her.

Tom unfolded himself from the tarp and stood up. The dog staggered to his feet and looked at Tom with questioning eyes. Tom patted his head.

"Come on, boy. It's safe now. You're comin' home with us." He climbed out of the boat and in a moment the dog clambered out behind him.

The rain was finally stopping and patches of blue were spreading across the sky. Back at the house Enoch found an old belt, measured it to the dog's neck, then cut it to size. "Now you've got a collar, big fella," he said, fastening it. Tom found a length of rope and they tied the dog to the fence. "This way he can't run away," Enoch said. "He'll need time to get used to our place."

Enoch looked the dog over, feeling his muscles and examining his teeth. "He seems healthy enough, and he's probably only a year old. His teeth are new and white."

"Give this to the dog." Fiona handed Tom a bone shank. "I made soup with it. It's still warm."

Tom gave the shank and a bowl of water to the dog. "Here you are, boy," he whispered. "You must be starvin'."

The dog lapped the water eagerly for a long time. Then he lay down, clamped the bone under his paw, and gnawed on it ravenously.

Enoch and Fiona watched from the porch.

"What will you name him?" Enoch asked.

Tom glanced thoughtfully at the dog, whose coat was as black as the sky had been that morning. "Let's call him Thunder," Tom said. "We found him in a thunderstorm."

"That jagged white streak on his chest reminds me of a lightnin' bolt," said Fiona.

"Aye! Thunder is the perfect name," Enoch agreed. "It's a puzzlement how the dog was out there in the sea with not another boat in sight. He must have been swimmin' for hours."

"Thank you for lettin' him stay with me," Tom said to Enoch.

Enoch's face became serious. "Remember, Tom. We must ask around for someone who's missin' a dog."

"Do you think we'll find the owner?"

"Hard to say. That dog came from somewhere. Still, the owners may be across the Atlantic by this time." Enoch came down from the porch and patted the dog's head. "But for now . . ."

"I know," Tom answered. "For now he's my very own dog." Tom hugged the wet animal. "You're my dream dog, Thunder," he whispered, "and we're goin' to have lots o' fun. I hopes I can keep you forever, boy!"

That afternoon Tom helped Enoch empty the load of fish from the skiff. Amos and Bert didn't show up until most of the work was done. Tom figured by their grumpy attitude that they both still carried a grudge about the dog.

Later Tom brought Thunder on the rope lead down to the flakes. The dog trotted ahead of him, pausing to sniff at the wind or head up a different path. Thunder would turn now and then, as if to make sure Tom was still there, and then walk briskly on.

When they reached the flakes they walked over wooden planks to the shanty where the women made fish, heading, boning, cleaning, and salting them, then dropping the guts into trunk holes to the water below. It was high tide and gulls screamed and fluttered overhead, diving for the castaway pieces of cod that floated out from under the wharves and stages.

Tom peered into the shanty. Fiona was inside with another woman. "Here's our Tom," Fiona said, wiping her hands on a rag. "Tom, meet Bert's mother, Ruby."

Ruby was a small, stout woman who looked like an older version of Nancy. "Hello, Tom. I've heard all about you . . . and that dog." She smiled ruefully. "So this is the animal that's causin' so much fuss." She put her hand out to Thunder, who sniffed at her fishy fingers. "Ah, he's lookin' for a bite to eat. Don't take my fingers, you big thing."

"It's all right, Thunder," said Fiona, patting the dog's head. "You'll get your share." She pointed to a pole outside. "Tie him up there, Tom. Then you can take these fish out to dry."

Tom tied Thunder's leash to the post. The dog lay down, put his head on his paws, and watched Tom spread the split cod in rows, head to tail, tail to head, as he had learned at the mission.

"Tom!" Nancy was standing nearby, her hands on her hips. "I hope you didn't forget. You're still goin' to teach me to read, aren't you?"

"I'll be pretty busy helpin' Enoch," Tom answered. "And I've got to take care of my dog now too."

"He's *not* your dog," Nancy reminded him. "And you promised you'd teach me!"

"I did not promise. Besides, you can't learn to read in one day. It takes time. And I don't have lots of time."

Nancy looked as if she were about to cry. "I want to read so bad." She turned to walk away.

"I'm sorry, Nancy," Tom called after her. "Maybe later . . . sometime."

"Never mind!" she yelled. "I don't want you to teach me anyways. You're nothin' but a . . . a stupid gommel!"

Tom watched her run up the plank to the road, and he knew she was crying.

"What's wrong, Nance?" Ruby called from the shack. But Nancy was already heading home. Ruby hurried after her daughter. "Wait, maid!" she called. "What's Tom done that's got you so upset?"

What *had* he done? There was already enough bad blood between him and Bert. Now Nancy, and probably Ruby, were angry with him too. Perhaps he should ask Enoch or Fiona if they could spare him once in a while to teach Nancy to read.

But how could he? If he told them about Nancy not being able to read, then he would betray his promise to keep Nancy's surprise.

There was more trouble ahead between the two families, and it was all Tom's fault!

Over the next few weeks Tom, Fiona, and Thunder headed out to the berry hills several times and filled buckets with blueberries, bakeapples, and partridgeberries. Fiona wore a bright calico skully on her head, with a wide brim that shaded her eyes and neck. Thunder, always by Tom's side, would stretch out in the sun. While Tom and Fiona bent over the shrubs and plucked the luscious fruit, dark-winged pitchy-paw butterflies floated around the bushes.

"Pitchy, pitchy better fly! If you don't, your mother will cry," Fiona sang.

After an hour or so of berry picking, Tom would stand and stretch and look out at the sapphire sea. It was a good place to be, here on Back o' the Moon Island. He looked forward to each morning and the caring and laughter he shared with the Murrays. Thunder was the dog he'd always wanted, and all his dreams of having a home were coming true.

He especially loved Saturday nights, when Enoch read from the Bible and the family would discuss the scriptures. Even Thunder was invited to join them. The dog would sit by Tom and rest his big head on Tom's leg while Tom patted him.

One night Fiona said, "Tom, you know a lot about the Bible."

"We read it every day at the mission," Tom told them. "And I memorized each of the Ten Commandments." He recited them off—all ten— without missing one.

They read about Jesus' resurrection of Lazarus. "He was such a dear friend of Jesus that Jesus cried when he heard Lazarus had died," Enoch noted.

"He'd been dead three days," Fiona added.

"Do you think Lazarus was in Heaven during that time?" Enoch asked Tom.

Tom thought about this. "I don't think so. If he were, he would have said something about it. If I'd been there I would have asked Lazarus, 'What was it like in Heaven?'"

"And if it was as glorious as they say, I would think Lazarus would have preferred to stay there." Fiona laughed.

"Jesus said that Lazarus was sleeping," Enoch said.

"So that must be what death is like." Tom was thoughtful and silent for a few minutes. Then he said, "It's nice to believe that my folks are asleep and will wake up again some day."

Fiona put her arm around him. "Ah, my child. In the meanwhile we're happy you're here, with us."

"I *am* happy here." Tom bent down to stroke Thunder and the dog lapped his face. Everyone laughed. "Thunder's happy here too," Tom said.

Tom figured he'd avoid Nancy until she had calmed down about those reading lessons. But Nancy seemed to have disappeared. Once or twice, though, Tom could have sworn he saw her peering out from the birches near the Murrays' house, or playing under the stages with little Rowena. Tom didn't see much of Bert, either, but when he did, he was usually with Eddie Rideout.

It was the middle of September now, and Fiona had been feeling poorly recently. On those days, Enoch went out to fish with Amos and Bert, while Tom stayed home to help her.

At night Tom tied Thunder to the fence, just until he got used to the place. In the morning the dog would whine and bark until Tom untied him. Then he followed Tom everywhere.

"He tags along after you like your own shadow," Fiona said from the couch where she was propped up with pillows. "Perhaps *Shadow* should have been his name."

"I love havin' him with me," Tom told her.

"I know," Fiona said. "Enoch has put up signs around Chance-Along to find Thunder's owner. He's tryin' to do what's right. But in my heart I want Thunder to stay with us."

"I hope we never find his true owner," Tom admitted.

One night at supper Enoch said, "That Amos is hard to work with. He has to have his own way. Can't seem to get over his grudge."

"He's still angry about the dog?" Fiona asked.

"Aye!" Enoch nodded. "I told him—I says, 'Amos, this game ain't worth the candle! Get over it!'"

"Is he still tryin' to find Thunder's owner?" Tom asked.

"That he is," Enoch said. "Each time he goes to Chance-Along, he makes it a point to ask sailors and fishermen if they're missin' a dog."

"But you've already done that," Fiona said. "You've put up signs and no one has responded. Why is Amos takin' this mission on himself?"

"I dunno. He's as hard to tell as the mind of a gull," Enoch answered.

"Ruby's actin' a bit offish too," Fiona replied. "She's hinted that someone has hurt Nancy's feelings."

Nancy's still upset with me about her reading lessons, Tom thought.

Later Tom sat out on the steps with Thunder and whispered in the dog's ear: "You and I have caused a lot o' bad feelings here in Back o' the Moon. But as long as we've got each other, we'll be okay, right, boy?" Thunder's tail wagged agreeably as he licked Tom.

Tom laughed and wiped his face. "Oh, you blubbery, wet thing!"

Still, Tom wished that he could make things better with the Bosworths. Since he was staying home with Fiona these days maybe he could find time to teach Nancy to read. Next time he saw her he'd tell her.

Meanwhile, Fiona lay on the couch and didn't eat much at all. During the day Tom would bring her a cup of tea or a biscuit with partridgeberry jam, which often soothed her stomach.

One afternoon Fiona decided to do laundry. "I can't leave this another day," she told Tom as she appeared with an armload of bedding. She heated water and Tom poured it into the washtub. Fiona began scrubbing with the yellow soap she had made herself from fat and lye.

When she finished, she said, "Tom, hang these out like a good boy."

Tom carried the heavy tub out to the clothesline which was strung between two crab apple trees. He began untwisting the shirts, socks, and trousers that Fiona had wrung out. He pinned underwear within pillowcases, as he was taught back at the orphanage. "No one wants to watch their underwear flappin' in the breeze for all to see," he'd been told.

"Look at the washwoman hangin' the clothes!" Bert stood nearby watching Tom with a sneer. He pointed to a pillowcase where Tom had hung Fiona's lace-trimmed panties. "Are those your pretty drawers under there?"

Tom wanted to haul off and smash Bert. Instead he tried to ignore the taunting words. "I thought you went out fishin' with Enoch and your father."

"Today I stayed home—not that it's any of your business."

"The laundry is none of your business either."

At this moment Thunder pounced around the corner of the house, barking excitedly.

"What is it, Thunder?" Tom asked as the dog leaped up, nearly knocking him over. "Stop it!" Thunder took hold of Tom's pants with his teeth, tugging and drawing Tom toward the front of the house.

"That's some wild dog!" Bert called. "You ain't trained him very well."

Thunder was frantic, barking and pulling at Tom. "All right, Thunder, I'm comin'. I'm comin'!" Tom ran after the excited dog, who raced ahead of him, leaving Bert standing by the clothesline, his arms across his chest impudently.

When Tom came around to the front porch he stopped in alarm. Fiona was sprawled on her back and her face white as snow.

"Fiona!" Tom screamed, bending over her. Was she breathing? He put his ear to her chest and could just hear her heart beating. Thunder stood by whining anxiously.

Tom ran into the house, grabbed a pillow, and darted outside. "Fiona!" he whispered, placing the pillow under her head. She moaned.

What should he do? Tom suddenly recalled the magical word charmers used to treat sick people. "Ananamazaptus! Ananamazaptus!" he whispered in Fiona's ear. But she didn't respond. "I shouldda known that wouldn't work! Just a lot o' pishogue!"

What to do? What to do? Enoch wasn't around, but maybe Ruby was. "Bert!" Tom called. "Get your ma! Fiona's fainted." Tom flew to the back of the house, and gasped. "That dirty squid!"

The clothesline and the clothes were all over the ground, and Bert was gone!

"Tom!" He heard Fiona calling and raced back to her. She was struggling to sit up.

"You fainted," he told her gently. "Keep your head down until you feel better." He remembered this from a first-aid course he had taken at the mission.

"I felt so weak," she said, sinking onto the pillow again. "Then I don't remember what happened."

"Did you hurt yourself when you fell?" Thunder sat down by Fiona and licked her face. "Thunder's the one who told me you needed help," Tom explained. "He came running and barking. That's how I found you."

"I'm all right now," Fiona said. "Just help me up to the porch chair."

Tom put his hands under her arms and lifted her to her feet. "You should stay quiet." Tom helped her slump into a rocker. Thunder sat by Fiona's side, thumping his tail, and gazed at her adoringly.

"What a fine, clever dog, you are," Fiona said,

scratching his neck. "We're glad you came to live with us." She looked at Tom, who was kneeling next to them. "We're right glad *you* came to live with us too, Tom."

Tom suddenly realized how very much he cared for Fiona . . . and Enoch as well. Now Fiona was ill. Her eyes seemed large in her pale, gaunt face. Tom had heard how very sick people, like his parents, seemed to just fade away and die with their illnesses. What if Fiona? . . .

Tom stood up. "I'll get you some tea," he said in a tremulous voice, "and a biscuit." He rushed into the house hoping Fiona didn't notice the tears he couldn't hold back.

"Dear Lord, please don't let anything happen to Fiona," Tom prayed.

When Enoch arrived home that evening he was distressed over Fiona's condition. "I'm takin' you to Dr. Sullivan at Chance-Along tomorrow," he insisted. "We've got to find out once and for all what's ailin' you, and why you're heavin' your stomach every day."

Tom helped Enoch get supper: cheese and ham scrambled with eggs, and slices of Fiona's fresh bread. Enoch insisted Fiona stay on the couch, and he carried a tray of food in to her. Tom and Enoch ate together in the kitchen.

After dinner Fiona decided to go to bed early. "Tom," she said as Enoch was helping her up the stairs, "be a good lad and bring in the dry clothes."

Tom had completely forgotten about the broken clothesline. All of Fiona's hard work was still lying on the ground. "I'll go right now," he said, heading for the back of the house. He was grateful that Fiona hadn't looked out the window.

Thunder followed Tom to the backyard. The early autumn breeze blew gently and cool. *It hadn't been a windy day*, Tom thought, *so the clothesline didn't fall in the wind*. Thunder sniffed at the clothes, then looked up at Tom questioningly.

After unpinning the clothes and putting them back in the tub, Tom examined the rope to see if it was frayed. It looked fairly new, and where it was broken it was not ragged at all. "It had to be Bert. This line was cut with a sharp knife," Tom muttered to Thunder.

"Are they dry?" Enoch asked when Tom came into the kitchen carrying the load of wash.

"No, they're dirty. Someone cut the clothesline, and I'll bet a dollar it was Bert."

"That cockabaloo! I have my bets on him too," Enoch exclaimed.

Tom set the tub on the table and began sorting the clothes from slightly dirty to very dirty. "Shall we wash them again?"

"We'll have to," said Enoch. "But we mustn't

tell Fiona. After all her work washing 'em, she'll be upset to see 'em like this."

Enoch pumped water into a big basin and fired up the stove again. "Looks like we've got our work cut out for us tonight," he said.

After the water was hot, Enoch poured it into the washtub. Tom and Enoch took turns scrubbing and wringing, and then they carried the laundry outside. Thunder sat and watched as Enoch tied the clothesline again. By the time they had finished hanging the clothes, it was dark. The moon was shining on the bay and down through the crab apple trees.

Enoch put his arm around Tom's shoulder. "Thank you, Tom, for taking fine care of Fiona."

"Thunder told me she had fainted," Tom said, patting the dog's head. "He was right crazy, barkin' and howlin' and pullin' at me."

"He's a special dog, that one," Enoch agreed, bending over to scratch Thunder's neck. "It was a blessin' findin' him out there in the sea." Enoch stood up. "I'd like to know for certain who cut that clothesline."

"It must've been Bert. He was here teasin' the

life out o' me 'cause I was hangin' clothes."

"Soon as I get a chance, I'm goin' to talk to Amos. There's been too much bad feelin' because of Thunder. Enough is enough." Enoch went inside.

Tom sat on the porch steps and buried his face in the soft fur around Thunder's neck. "I wonder if Bert ever did mean things to the Murrays before I arrived."

Were all these bad things happening because of *him*?

The next morning Thunder was not tied to the fence waiting for Tom. Where was he? Tom walked around the house, but there was no sign of the dog. "He'll show up," Enoch said. Still, Tom had a sinking feeling.

Enoch and Tom helped Fiona into the boat for their trip to the doctor. "It'll be shorter to go by boat than to take the horse and cart over the bumpy roads." Enoch started up the engine, and Tom unhitched the ropes.

"Shall I come too?" Tom asked.

"Why don't you stay and keep an eye on things,"

Enoch said. "And you can look for Thunder."

"I will." Tom smiled at Fiona. "I hope you're goin' to be all right."

"I'll be fine," Fiona assured him. "Thank you, child."

Tom watched as the boat pulled away and headed to the shore across Rumble Reach. Then he flew up the steps of the stages to the high ground, where the Murrays' house stood. "Thunder! Thunder!" He raced out to the chicken coop where Rufus, feathers ruffled, crowed and chased after him, pecking at his legs.

Tom checked the yard and shed, then dashed out back along the path to the tuckamore and berry bushes. "Thunder! Thunder!"

Once, when he thought he heard a bark, he stopped, listening. But the only sound was the echo of his own voice as he called his dog's name, and the shuffle of dry autumn leaves in the wind.

Finally Tom went to the backyard to take in the laundry. He looked toward the opposite shore and wondered how Fiona was doing and whether the doctor could really help her. "Please, please, make Fiona well," Tom prayed.

On his way back to the house, Tom paused by the fence and noticed that Thunder's rope was gone. It wasn't likely the rope had become unfastened—it had been tied with a strong knot. Had someone undone it and taken Thunder away? Bert?

Tom decided to walk over to the Bosworths to confront Bert. After all, he had cut the clothesline. Tom was sure of that. And Bert had wanted the dog badly. Yes, he was going over there right now.

After depositing the tub of clothes in the kitchen, Tom went down the side of the hill, through the flakes, to the shore road where the Bosworths lived. As he approached the tall green house he saw Nancy swinging under a tree with little Rowena on her lap.

"Hey, Nancy. Have you seen Thunder?" he yelled. But Nancy didn't answer. She leaped off the swing and pulled a screaming Rowena into the house with her.

Ruby poked her head out the door. "Did you lose Thunder, boy?" Tom could see Nancy watching him from behind the curtains.

"Have you seen him?"

"No, I ain't seen him," Ruby answered. "How's

Fiona? Has she gone to the doctor yet?"

"She's there now," Tom answered. "Where's Bert?"

"Out somewhere. Maybe helpin' Amos down on the flakes." Ruby went inside.

Tom hadn't seen Bert or Amos when he passed the flakes earlier. After a moment's deliberation, he headed back to his house. Thunder knew where he was fed and loved. Perhaps he'd have come back already.

As Tom climbed the road to the high land, he began to worry about Fiona again. She and Enoch should be back this afternoon. Even though it was still too early for their return, Tom looked anxiously out to the mainland, watching for any signs of Enoch's white skiff.

Tom picked the last of the summer daisies that grew by the side of the road. He'd surprise Fiona with them. He'd surprise her too by putting away the clean clothes.

He reached the gate to the Murrays' yard. Once more he called, "Thunder! Come home, boy." But there was no sign of the dog.

. . .

The sun was about to set when Tom heard the sound of an engine in the harbor. He looked out and saw Enoch's skiff as it putted up to the wharf.

The door slammed behind Tom as he ran outside and darted down the hillside path to the lower road. Enoch had already tied up the boat, and Fiona was on to the dock when Tom arrived, out of breath.

Fiona was smiling and her eyes sparkled. Her face seemed less pale—even rosy from the trip across the harbor. "Hello, Tom," she said.

"Is everything all right?"

Fiona put her arms around him. "Don't worry about me so much, lad." She looked over at Enoch, who stood by watching them.

"What did the doctor say?" Tom asked Fiona. "Are you well?"

"I'll tell you all 'bout it," she answered. "But right now I'm tired and I'm goin' to lie down."

Somethin' isn't right, Tom thought. *Somethin' they're not tellin' me.*

enoch helped Fiona out of her sweater and onto the couch. "Fiona has something to tell you," he said to Tom.

Fiona patted the sofa cushions, beckoning Tom to sit by her. He walked slowly, his heart pounding, then sat down and looked into her gray eyes. Was she going to die? Like his mother? A lump grew in his throat and he could hardly ask, "What's wrong?"

"Tom," she said, taking his hand. "There's nothing wrong at all. In fact, it's something wonderful. I'm goin' to have a baby!"

A baby!

Fiona went on. "We can hardly believe it! After all these years . . ."

"A baby." Tom finally spoke. "When?"

"In the spring. April! That's why I've been feeling so ill, you see."

Tom had heard that women in a family way sometimes felt sick. He was relieved that Fiona wasn't going to die. But now a strange new emotion came over him—something he couldn't quite figure out. It wasn't joy, like he should be feeling. It was sadness. But, why?

"Will you be all right?" Tom asked. "I mean . . . the doctor is so far away. . . ."

"That's true. But we have Margaret Rideout up the road. She's a granny—a midwife. She delivered Nancy Bosworth and lots of other babies over the years. I'm sure she'll be happy to help me, too."

Enoch said, "We need to celebrate, Tom! Shall we make a cake or something for supper?"

Tom nodded and stood up. "I'll raise the fire." He went to the kitchen, opened the drafts, then added scraps of wood. The fire began to blaze. Tom poured water into the kettle, put it on the stove, and sank into a kitchen chair.

He could hear Enoch and Fiona speaking in soft words.

Enoch peeked in. "Are you all right, son?"

"I'm fine," Tom said. But he wasn't fine. He wished Thunder were around. He could tell Thunder how he was feeling. "I . . . I'm worried about Thunder is all. I'm afraid he's gone for good." Suddenly he raced out of the kitchen and up the stairs to his bedroom.

"Tom? Tom? What's wrong?" Fiona called after him.

Tom fell on the bed and gathered his pillow close to him. Things were happening too fast. He was just beginning to feel like part of this family and now . . . what?

His thoughts were interrupted by a knock on the door. "Tom, may I come in?" Fiona asked.

Tom sat up. "Yes, please."

Fiona stood in the doorway carrying a lantern. Tom hadn't realized how dark it had become. "Tom, we'll find Thunder. If he's gone for good, we'll get you another dog. I promise."

"But I don't want another dog," Tom said quietly.

Fiona placed the lantern on the bureau, then sat on Tom's bed. "Is somethin' else botherin' you?"

"No. I'm happy for you and Enoch, that you'll

have a baby in the spring." He suddenly realized what was hurting him so badly. "You w-won't want me gettin' in the way . . . ," he stammered. "I mean, you won't need me now that . . ."

Fiona gathered him into her arms. "We'll always want you and need you," she whispered as he laid his head against her. "And the baby will love and need you too."

This was a new dream—one he had never considered. He suddenly pictured himself as an older brother, helping to feed the baby, watching the baby laugh, and holding him—or her.

"Does Enoch want me to stay too?"

"Of course he does."

Tom sighed. "I'm glad," he said.

"I'm goin' to search everywhere for Thunder today," Tom announced the next morning. "He's got to be *somewhere* on this island."

"You go on," Enoch said. "I'll go down to the flakes and ask Amos about it. And I want to ask that Bert if he knows anythin' about our clothes-line."

Tom headed up the road to the back meadow

where Prince was grazing. "Thunder!" Tom called. The horse looked up and then went back to chewing the tall grass.

Tom crossed the field toward an old, unpainted barn. Grasshoppers tickled his legs and the sun beat down like July instead of late September. He began to run through the grass toward the barn, when he heard someone call his name. "Tom!" It was Nancy. "Wait!"

He stopped as Nancy caught up to him. "Where are you goin'?" she asked.

"I'm lookin' for my dog. Do you know where he is?"

"Um, maybe."

"What do you mean 'maybe'?"

Nancy folded her arms across her chest. "If I tell you where Thunder is, will you do somethin' for me?"

"What?"

"You told me you'd teach me to read and then you went back on your word."

"Come on, Nancy. I never promised any such thing. Where's my dog?"

"If I tell you, will you teach me to read?"

"Um . . . all right."

Nancy's eyebrows furrowed into a worried frown. "You've got to swear you won't tell anyone how you found out where Thunder is."

"I swear!" Tom said impatiently. "Now, where *is* Thunder?"

"He's in the barn, the one in the far meadow." She gestured to the crumbling barn in the distance.

"I was about to look there anyway," Tom said as Nancy scurried away. "Thunder!" he shouted as he headed across the pasture toward the barn. This time he heard a muffled bark. Running, Tom called again, and as he got closer the excited barks were clearer. It had to be Thunder!

The barn door was latched with a piece of lumber. Tom lifted the board and the door opened. The smell of hay drifted from the dark interior. "Thunder?" He could hear whining and scratching. "Thunder!"

A joyous bark answered him from a stall on the opposite side of the barn. Tom ran through the darkness and threw open the door of the stall. The black dog leaped up, nearly knocking Tom over, lapping his face and whining happily.

"Oh, my good boy," Tom shouted, laughing. "I found you. I found you!"

A shadow appeared in the open doorway. It was Bert.

t om noticed the rope that bound Thunder to the stall was the one that had disappeared from the Murrays'. "I'm takin' Thunder home where he belongs, Bert."

"No! You had him for a month," Bert argued. "Now it's *my* turn."

"Who said we were goin' to take turns?"

Bert grabbed for Thunder's collar, but Tom pushed him away. "You have no right to steal Thunder from me!"

Bert pushed him back. "How could I steal him from you? You don't own him!" He shoved Tom again.

"Keep your hands off o' me!" Tom warned.

"No, I won't! Take this!" Bert pulled his arm back and then slammed his fist into Tom's chest.

Thunder growled and barked excitedly.

Tom's anger was stronger than the pain. He dove at Bert, tackling him to the ground. As he landed, Tom heard the crunch of glass. *His pocket watch!* Now he was furious. He went after Bert, his fists pounding at his chest and face.

Barking, Thunder circled the boys as they pummeled each other. Bert struggled to his feet and was about to kick Tom when Thunder grabbed the leg of Bert's trousers with his teeth and pulled him away from Tom.

"Better stay away from me, Bert. Thunder might bite your head off!" Tom said. "He's decided who he wants to be with . . . and it isn't you!" He brushed himself off and headed out of the barn with Thunder by his side.

"I don't want that ugly ol' dog!" Bert yelled after them. "You won't get to keep him anyway. My pa's goin' to find the real owner if it's the last thing he does on this earth!"

When Tom and Thunder came around the final bend in the road back home, Fiona went out to meet them. "Well, lo and behold you, Thunder," she said, opening the gate. "Where have you been?" She bent down and patted the dog, who licked her hand.

"Bert hid him in the barn out in the back meadow."

"My blessed fortune! What happened to you?" Fiona brushed the dirt from Tom's hair. "Did you have a fight with Bert?"

Tom nodded. "He said his pa's gonna find Thunder's owner and take him away from us." He reached into his pocket and brought out the gold watch. The cover was dented, the glass on the face was smashed, and the screw that wound the watch was broken off.

"Oh, Tom! What's this?" Fiona put her hand out and Tom dropped the broken timepiece into her palm.

"My pocket watch. It belonged to my grand-father and then my father," Tom said. "I've kept it like somethin' precious all this time. I even sleep with it under my pillow. And now it's ruined. That's what I get for fightin' with Bert." Tom swallowed hard, holding back tears.

Fiona put her arm around him. "I'll see if we can get it fixed somewhere." She pulled a handkerchief from her pocket and wrapped the broken watch carefully. "Maybe when Enoch goes to St. John's." She noticed a tear on his cheek and brushed it away. "It'll be all right, my child. You'll see. Enoch should be back from talking to Amos anytime now." Fiona went into the house. "Thunder, you must be hungry. I'll get you some nice leftover stew."

Tom sat on the steps, his chin cupped in his hands. Thunder sat next to him, watching him with curious eyes. Would Enoch really be able to make things better with Amos? "I feel like a jinker," Tom said to Thunder. "I've brought nothin' but bad luck since I came."

Thunder leaned against Tom. "We're both orphans, Thunder," Tom said. "Don't you ever leave me again. We need to stick together no matter what."

Fiona came onto the porch with a big dish of leftovers. "Here you are, Thunder. A welcome home feast!" She set it on the porch floor and Thunder gobbled it up, his tail swishing happily.

Fiona sat down with Tom on the steps just as Enoch appeared coming up the road.

"What happened with Amos?" Fiona asked when he came through the gate.

"Amos was pretty sore at me for makin' such a to-do about Bert's pranks." Enoch scratched the back of his head. "He says the dog's a jinx—he's brought nothin' but bad luck."

"That's pishogue!" Fiona snapped. "Bad luck, indeed!"

"I told him we're keepin' Thunder. In fact, I tore down the notices we put up about a missing dog." He stroked Thunder's ears. "We've had those signs up for well over a month now and no one's responded. O' course, I don't know how many notices Amos sent out to other ports or fisheries. But as far as I'm concerned the dog is yours, Tom."

Tom threw his arms around Thunder. "Hear that? You're my dog, good and true!"

Fiona frowned. "I don't trust Amos. He's carryin' such a grudge, no tellin' what he might do."

"He'll be all right," Enoch assured her, "once this has all blown over."

Fiona was beginning to feel better, and for the next several days, Tom and Enoch and Thunder went fishing by themselves. It was a quiet and pleasant time, and Enoch told Tom stories of the sea. Tom especially liked the stories of pirates, like Peter Easton, the "Pirate Admiral" who captured three Spanish treasure ships and divided the bounty with his crew. According to legend, he and other pirates hid their treasures in some of the caves along the Newfoundland shoreline. "They timed the opening of the caves with the tides," Enoch explained. "Only for a few moments during the day could the caves be entered. And no one knows, of the thousands of caves along the cliffs, which might contain the treasures."

Tom had quiet times too. He'd row along the shoreline in his little red punt. Thunder sat in the bow, sniffing at the water or barking at a bird. Sometimes they'd hike toward Eastern Head, peering into the caves that were tucked into the crags and wondering about pirates and treasures.

One October morning, as he and Thunder were exploring the high ground near Eastern Head and climbing across the enormous boulders, Tom heard something. Thunder heard it too, as he stopped with his ears flicked up, listening.

Then Tom saw it: a large cave in the cliff. A strange high-pitched, squeaky voice drifted out from within the dark opening.

"**a**yedisismeveryowncopy'ouseandnoonecan-
enterlessisayso!"

It was Nancy! She and Rowena were standing by the open cave!

"What were you singin'?" he asked. "Cheek music?"

"It's jannie talk," Rowena piped up.

"You know, like the mummers—the jannies," Nancy said. "They come to houses at Christmastime in their masks and talk their silly jannie talk."

Tom had heard of the mummers when he lived at the mission, but had never seen them. He had been told they wore crazy costumes and showed up at Christmastime in an old Newfoundland custom. They were considered too rowdy and wild, so they were often unwelcome. Tom knew they spoke in weird voices with strange messages to disguise themselves.

"I can't tell what Nancy's sayin' when she talks jannie talk," Rowena said. "She says she's speakin' with real words, but I don't believe her."

"Tom! Come see our copy house," Nancy said. "It's our own secret place, and you can't tell anyone."

"Why would I?" Tom stepped into the cave and was surprised to see how well the girls' playhouse was hidden in the wall of the cliff. A flat rock was set like a table with pieces of shard. A doll wrapped in a blanket was tucked into a depression which looked very much like a cradle. It was crowded in the cave, so Tom went outside again.

"Listen here, Tom," Nancy said, following him. "This is the place where you can teach me to read. Wait!" She went back into the shallow cave and brought out a canvas envelope. "I have paper, pencils, and a brand new notebook my aunt sent me. We can sit outside, or if it gets cold, we can go into the cave. So sit down right now and help me. You promised." She sat on a smooth boulder and pulled Rowena into her lap.

Tom sat next to them while Thunder lay down by his feet. "Do you know your alphabet?"

"I know my alphabet," Rowena chimed in. "A, B, C, D . . . ," she sang.

"Hush!" Nancy silenced her, and then answered. "I know the alphabet from A to Zed. But I don't know how to make words with the letters."

"Every letter has a sound, sometimes more than one sound," Tom told her. "There are five vowels you need to learn." He wrote A E I O U in the notebook, one vowel on each page. He explained each vowel and its sounds. "Say 'aaah, ay,'" he showed her, beginning with the letter A.

Nancy repeated the sounds after Tom. Little Rowena tried too. "Those aren't words, Tom," Nancy protested.

"But they're like . . . magic ingredients," Tom said.

"Magic?" Rowena's eyes widened.

"They make the other letters become words. You'll see." Tom pointed to the vowels. "Practice all these sounds, and the next time I'll show you how they make words." He got up to leave.

"When's the next time? Tomorrow?"

"All right. I'll be here tomorrow at the same time."

Several mornings during the next few weeks Tom met Nancy and Rowena at the cave. Thunder always went along with him. Enoch was still fishing with Amos until the winter ice came in and closed the harbor. Since Fiona was feeling better, Tom was free to give Nancy her lessons. Tom was surprised how quickly Nancy learned. But Rowena was distracting, whining for attention or wandering off among the rocks. Thunder always sprawled out in a sunny spot and slept, snoring now and then.

One day Tom spent a longer time than usual, showing Nancy how changing just one letter can change a word. "Take the word *cat*," he explained to Nancy. "See how you can change it by switching the first letter?"

"Bat!" Nancy said, pointing to the letter B. "H . . . hat!"

"Good for you, Nancy," Tom praised her. He got up. "I've got to go back and see if Fiona needs me. Try writing all the '*at*' words you can think of, and I'll see them when I come back."

"All right," Nancy agreed.

Thunder pulled himself up and followed Tom.

Rowena was climbing a boulder toward the tuckamore at the top of the slope. "You'd better keep an eye on Rowena," Tom said. "She could wander away."

Nancy nodded, already busy writing words in her notebook.

When Tom and Thunder arrived home, the house smelled of cinnamon and apples, and a crackling fire burned in the wood stove.

"I baked muffins this morning!" Fiona said. "Sit down and have one with me, Tom." She poured tea for the two of them and spread bakeapple jam on the steaming muffins.

Tom removed his jacket and sat at the table. "These are right scrumptious," Tom said, his mouth full.

Fiona sipped her tea. "Where do you go on your mornin' walks, Tom?"

"Up beyond the Bosworths' house, but not all the way to Eastern Head. Just up to where the boulders are."

"What do you and Thunder do up there all by yourselves?"

He put down his teacup. "Can I tell you a secret?"

"Of course."

"I've been teachin' Nancy Bosworth how to read."

"Oh, aye! That's right nice of you, boy," Fiona said. "Does her mother know?"

"Oh, no, Nancy doesn't want me to tell anyone yet. It's goin' to be a surprise for her folks."

"It's plain to see that Ruby and Bert can't read."

"Nancy said that her ma pretends she can." Tom grinned. "Bert makes believe he can too. He spells *fish* C-O-D."

Fiona laughed, sputtering her tea and muffin. "Too bad Bert doesn't join you for lessons." She tapped at her mouth with a serviette.

"He's too proud to ask for help, 'specially from me."

"Pride goeth before a fall," Fiona quoted.

At that moment Thunder began to bark from the porch.

"Fiona! Fiona! Come quick!"

Fiona opened the door. Ruby stood there, as pale as a ghost, her hair a messy slattery-sling. Nancy was sobbing behind her.

"What's wrong, Ruby?" Fiona asked.

"It's Rowena—she's gone!"

"She just disappeared!" Nancy cried hysterically. "I'm afeard the fairies took her!"

"Rowena's mother is at the cave with Bert and Eddie," Ruby said. "They're searchin' for her. Come down, Tom. We need all the help we can get!"

"I'll be back in a spurt," Tom told Fiona as he grabbed his jacket. "No need for you to come and climb over the rocks." Tom raced outside and down the road with Thunder at his heels. When they approached the boulders, Tom could see Bert and Eddie searching the shoreline. Rowena's mother, Margaret, was near the cave, screaming "Rowena!" She held the little girl's doll in her hand.

"I'll go up to the tuckamore," Tom told Margaret.

"I don't think she'd climb all the way up there." She wept.

"I was watchin' her every second," Nancy insisted, biting her lip. "I'm sure the fairies came and took her!"

"Fairies?" Ruby whacked Nancy on her rump. "Don't blame the fairies. You weren't watchin' her like you were s'posed to!"

"I hope she didn't fall down among the rocks somewhere," Margaret sobbed. "She may be hurt or bleedin'. . . ."

Tom took the doll from Margaret's hands. "Here, Thunder." He held it to Thunder's nose. "Find Rowena!" he ordered. The dog sniffed at the doll then looked at Tom. "Go! Get Rowena!" Tom said again. "Go!"

Thunder sniffed around the entrance to the cave. He gave a slight bark and then headed up the rocks and into the spruce forest. Tom followed as Thunder pushed his way through thick trees. Briars and needles stuck to his fur, and to Tom's jacket. "Rowena!" Tom called. But there was no answer.

Thunder stopped. Tom held the doll to his nose again. Thunder sniffed it and then went on.

They had gone a long way—high up on the cliffs of Eastern Head. Tom went to the edge of the cliff and looked down. The sea, hundreds of feet beneath him, broke in waves against the rocks. If Rowena fell from here . . .

Tom peered once more at the deep sea and the jagged rocks below. "We've *got* to find her," he said to Thunder.

Tom recalled Nancy's insistence that the fairies took Rowena. Superstitions from old Scotland and Ireland still had a hold on some people. Tom found himself wondering if the fairies really *had* taken Rowena!

Pishogue! he told himself.

Thunder continued on through the brush, his nose close to the ground. Then, suddenly they came to a clearing. The sun shone into the opening and cast a glow on a mossy nook. And there was Rowena, curled up on the soft moss, sound asleep. Thunder's tail wagged furiously as he trotted over to the little girl and licked her face. Rowena stirred and woke up, wiping the dried tears from her eyes. "Thunder," she whimpered, throwing her arms around his neck. "I got lost!"

Tom sighed with relief, then handed her the doll. "You're safe now, my child," he said. "Thunder found you. He knew exactly where you were." He took Rowena's hand and led her out of the thicket. "Let's go back. Everyone's lookin' for you."

When they arrived at the cave, they saw Margaret and Ruby racing up the rocks. "Oh, thank God!" Margaret screamed when she saw Rowena. She ran to her daughter and clasped her close.

"She wandered off into the woods," Tom explained. "Thunder went straight to her."

"Thank you, Thunder," Margaret said, patting the dog with one hand and clinging to Rowena with the other.

Bert and Eddie climbed up to the cave. "Where was she?"

"Thunder found her," Tom said. "She was asleep up in the tuckamore."

Ruby turned to Nancy. "How did this happen? You were supposed to be watching her."

Nancy's eyes filled with tears. "I'm sorry. I was readin' . . . and she just went off."

"Readin'?" Ruby raised her eyebrows. "You can't read."

"Tom is teachin' me," Nancy told her. "I was goin' to surprise you."

"And what was Rowena doin' while you were reading, Miss High 'n' Mighty?" Ruby scolded her daughter. "Watchin' Rowena is more important than learnin' to read. And you should know that too, Tom."

"Tom told me to keep an eye on Rowena," Nancy blurted out. "It's not his fault."

"Leave them be," Margaret said to Ruby. "Tom and Thunder found Rowena, and everything is all right now."

"It won't happen again," Nancy promised. "I'm real sorry. . . ."

Ruby crossed her arms and glared at Tom. "I don't want you teachin' Nancy to read. It's already caused enough problems."

"But, Mama, I'm doin' real good with my readin'. Aren't I, Tom?"

Tom nodded. "She learns real quick."

Ruby grabbed her daughter by the arm. "There'll be no more talk about readin'! You're gettin' too big for your britches even thinkin' about it."

"I could teach you and Bert, too, Mrs. Bosworth." Tom bit his lip, suddenly remembering that no one was supposed to know Ruby couldn't read.

The woman turned on him, her face flushed. "I don't need *you* to teach me anything, Tom Campbell!"

"And I don't need you either," Bert added crossly.

"Don't be so hard on Tom," Margaret objected. "Everything's all right."

"True. But if it hadn't been for him and his highfalutin ideas, Rowena wouldn't have got lost in the first place!" Ruby stomped off between the boulders, shoving Nancy ahead of her.

"Thank you for bringing Rowena back safely, Tom." Margaret patted Thunder's smooth head. "You're a right clever dog, Thunder."

Bert and Eddie were whispering to each other. Before they walked away, Eddie said, "We want to talk to you later, Tom."

"Yeah," Bert echoed. "We've got to talk." They climbed over the boulders and caught up with their mothers.

Tom and Thunder stayed behind as the others made their way back to the road.

"Looks like I'm in trouble with the Bosworths again, Thunder," Tom said. But when he looked up, he smiled. Little Rowena had turned to wave good-bye and was throwing kisses to them both.

that night Fiona and Tom told Enoch the news about Thunder's great rescue of Rowena.

"The day we found that dog, God was shinin' his blessing on us," Enoch said.

"Amos still says he brought nothin' but trouble," Tom reminded them.

"Trouble! He brought you to me when I fell, and now he's saved Rowena," Fiona declared. "Thunder's a godsend, that's what he is."

"Bert says his pa's still tryin' to find Thunder's real owner."

"Just to spite us." Fiona threw her hands up. "It's not out of the goodness of his heart; you can be sure of that!"

Tom recalled Bert and Eddie's last words to

him. *We want to talk with you.* He wondered what they were up to next.

Out on the porch Thunder began to bark. Margaret Rideout was at the door with Rowena and Eddie. "We've got somethin' for you and Thunder," she said when Tom opened it.

With a grin, Eddie handed Tom a plate of ginger cookies. "Thanks for findin' my sister."

"It was Thunder who found her," Tom said.

Margaret came inside and put a paper-wrapped package on the kitchen table. "This is a nice hard lamb bone for Thunder. I left a good bit o' meat on it too. He deserves it." She nudged Rowena. "What do you have to say, maid?"

"Thank you for findin' me, Tom."

"And my Eddie has somethin' to say too," Margaret said.

Eddie shuffled his feet and his face flushed. "Um, Tom . . . could you help me with my readin' sometime?"

"We think it's wonderful that you've been helpin' Nancy. Eddie's had a little book learnin', but not enough," Margaret said. "We'd find some way to pay you back, Tom."

"I probably shouldn't tell you this," Eddie said sheepishly. "Bert says he wants to read too."

For a moment Tom was speechless. Was that what Bert wanted to talk to him about? "Sure, Eddie. I'll be glad to help both of you."

Fiona spoke up. "Oh, Tom, how good of you not to hold resentment against Bert after all he's done."

"We're right proud of you, son," Enoch added.

Margaret smiled in agreement. "Why don't you come to our house to do schoolwork?" Margaret suggested. "It's gettin' too cold out at the caves. Or you can use the old church down by the bridge. Might as well put it to some good use."

Rowena tugged at her mother's arm. "I know my ABCs." And she began singing.

Everyone laughed. "Bring Thunder inside, Tom, and give him his bone," Fiona said. "Then we'll all have a cup of hot tea."

The following morning Fiona asked, "Tom, want to come to Chance-Along with us? I'm goin' to see the doctor this morning. We're takin' the wagon."

"Can we bring Thunder?"

"'Course we can!"

After breakfast Enoch harnessed Prince to the wagon, and they piled in. Thunder and Tom sat in the back as the carriage bounced over the rutty roads. It was November now. The trees were bare except for the firs. The air was cold, and Tom huddled in the woolen jacket and hat that had been handmade at the mission.

They passed the neglected church with its old steeple stretching up into the blue sky. The wooden bridge rattled as they crossed over, and then the road became wider and busier. Thunder sat tall, sniffing the crisp air. He seemed to smile as he gazed about, watching the sights of the town.

"Look over there!" Enoch called, and pointed out an automobile. "I heard one of those motor cars was brought over from Nova Scotia . . . and there it is!"

"It's a beauty!" Tom exclaimed. The maroon auto, with its polished nickel trim, made its way through the pedestrians and horses. The driver waved and honked the horn to onlookers. Thunder stood up and barked.

"There's the lawyer, Mr. Robinson, at the helm," Enoch said. "He's the only one in town with money enough to own an automobile."

The car stopped by the Murrays' wagon. "Say, Enoch!" Mr. Robinson called.

Enoch pulled on Prince's reins. "Good morrow to you, Mr. Robinson. Come over and meet our boy, Tom Campbell here, and his dog, Thunder."

The man got out of his motor car and approached the wagon. "Hello, Tom," he said genially. "How do you like livin' with the Murrays? They'll be good to you, you can bet your britches."

"They are good to me, sir," Tom said. "They've made me feel right welcome."

"And this is the wonder dog," the man said, scratching Thunder's head. "Found 'im out on the sea, I hear tell."

"Besides himself, he saved me, and Rowena Rideout as well," Fiona told him.

"Aye! Ken Rideout told me all about it when he came in town this mornin'," said Mr. Robinson.

"I heard Amos Bosworth's been tryin' to find the real owner of this dog."

"Have you heard anything about an owner?" Enoch asked. Tom held his breath.

"No. N'arn a word," Mr. Robinson answered.

"It'd be a shame if we lost him," Fiona said.

"Now, Enoch," Mr. Robinson said as he headed back to his automobile, "you've got a boy and a dog, and a baby comin' soon. Pretty good for a man who had no family for so long!"

"Good things come to him who waits," Enoch quoted with a laugh. "We'll be seein' you soon!" He clicked the reins and they moved on, turning onto a road to the left that led down to the waters of Rumble Reach. After about a mile, they came to a tan-colored house set on a hillside. Prince stopped by the fence, and Enoch helped Fiona out of the wagon. "Come with us and meet Dr. Sullivan," Fiona said to Tom. "He probably won't deliver our baby. But while we can get here easily, before the snows come, it's a good idea to see the doctor— just to make sure everything's goin' right."

Tom climbed out of the back of the wagon. "Stay here, Thunder. Stay!" The dog, who had been about to follow Tom, settled down obediently.

Dr. Sullivan came to the door and shook hands with everyone. "Come in, Fiona," he said, "and let's see how this baby is doin'."

Tom and Enoch sat on chairs in the waiting room while Fiona went inside. Enoch handed Tom a month-old copy of the St. John's newspaper, but Tom couldn't concentrate on it. He wondered about Fiona and the baby. He could hear the doctor's deep voice, and Fiona's soft answers, but he couldn't make out what they were saying.

After a while the office door opened and Dr. Sullivan peered out. "Enoch, my boy. How would you like to hear the baby's heartbeat?" The doctor laughed at Enoch's dumbfounded expression. "I've recently purchased the very latest, most powerful stethoscope. Got it straight from McGill University in Montreal. If you aren't scared or embarrassed, you can come in and listen. After all, it's your baby too." Enoch nodded and followed the doctor into the examining room.

Tom sat alone, filled with awe and wonder. Imagine! The baby isn't even born and they're listening to its heartbeat. Somehow it didn't seem like a real baby—after all, there wasn't anything to see—'cept for Fiona's belly getting rounder.

His thoughts were interrupted when Enoch opened the door. "Tom, Fiona wants you to come in too—if you'd like, that is." He turned to the doctor. "I'm not sure. . . . After all, he's just a boy."

"Let Tom come," Fiona called. "It's a wondrous thing to share with him."

Tom stood up, dropping the newspaper from his lap.

"Are you all right with this, Tom?" Enoch asked.

"Oh, yes," Tom stammered. "I'm all right." He followed Enoch timidly, and blushed when he saw Fiona lying on a table, a white sheet over her pudgy stomach.

"Don't be shy, Tom. It's a beautiful thing to know there's a real live baby growin' inside," Fiona assured him.

"Maybe you'll be a doctor someday," Dr. Sullivan said to Tom as he moved the stethoscope over the sheet that covered Fiona's belly. "Right here," he said, holding the scope steady. "You'll hear Fiona's heart the loudest. But if you listen carefully, you'll hear the baby's heart. It's much faster than Fiona's and very faint." He put the instrument into Tom's ears.

Tom closed his eyes, concentrating. As the doctor said, he could hear Fiona's heart thumping, but there were other sounds too, like gurgling water and the whishing sound of Fiona's breath. Then he heard a faint pitter-patter, like the flutter of a hummingbird's wings.

"I hear it!" Tom said. "I can hear our baby's heartbeat!"

tom's face flushed. It had been bigheaded for him to say "our baby." This wasn't really *his* family. He was still only a visitor, a guest. He stepped back from Fiona and turned away.

"Enoch, you and Tom go back to the waiting room while Fiona gets dressed," Dr. Sullivan told them. "Everything is coming along just fine. And you've got Margaret Rideout out there on the island who's an excellent granny, in case you can't get back to me in April when the baby's due."

Fiona nodded. "Margaret's delivered a lot of babies. I'm sure I'll be in capable hands."

After Enoch did some errands, the family ate lunch at the Copper Kettle, a charming restaurant near the docks. Tom tied Thunder to a pile by the window so he could watch the dog while they ate. Tom had never been to a real restaurant. He tried to remember his best manners. "It's right pretty in here," he said, looking around at the shiny brass lanterns on each table, and the red valances on the windows.

There were so many choices on the menu that Tom couldn't make up his mind. He finally decided on a beef and vegetable pie and fresh milk to drink. Back on the island they only had canned milk.

After lunch Tom took Thunder for a walk through the town of Chance-Along while Enoch and Fiona did errands. Some people who had heard about Thunder's good deeds stopped to pet him. "Oh, this is the dog that found the little Rideout girl," one woman said. "You're a hero, aren't you, boy? A real hero." She scratched Thunder's neck. The dog enjoyed the attention and wagged his tail vigorously.

It was late afternoon when they returned to Back o' the Moon. They crossed the wooden bridge to the island. The old church was just ahead. At this moment Thunder leaped out of the wagon, raced ahead, then stopped directly in front of Prince. Prince halted and pawed the ground uneasily while the dog barked.

"What's wrong?" Fiona asked.

"Get outta the way, Thunder!" Enoch clicked the reins. "Giddap, Prince!"

Prince's ears flattened and his nostrils flared. Skittish, he thumped his feet and neighed. But Thunder stayed in the horse's path and howled.

Tom climbed out of the wagon. "What's wrong, Thunder?" he asked, trying to pull the dog out of the horse's way. But Thunder resisted, his paws firmly planted on the road. "Get out of the way, Thunder!" Tom ordered. He pulled Thunder's collar again, but this time Thunder sat down.

"He'll move when Prince gets closer. Giddap!" Enoch commanded, snapping the reins. Tom jumped aside as Prince started forward with a jolt. Suddenly the ground rumbled and shook violently. The horse reared and tried to run, but Thunder still barred his way, barking and circling.

"It's an earthquake!" Enoch yelled.

"Oh, Blessed Savior!" Fiona screamed. "What'll we do?"

Tom ran to Thunder and threw his arms around him. An earthquake! He'd heard of terrible earthquakes in other parts of the world, but never heard of one in Newfoundland.

The land around them rolled, like the waves of the sea, uprooting trees and fences.

"Look at the church!" Enoch yelled.

The family watched in terror as the church shook violently. The steeple tottered, and then crumbled to the ground with a crash and the somber clangs of the church bell. Just ahead a rut deepened, then opened into a large furrow, spanning the entire roadway. The rumbling slowed, rattled again, then stopped.

"Our house!" Fiona wailed. "Is it still standing?"

"We'll go on home and find out, my girl," Enoch's voice was comforting as he put his arms around her. "We'll be all right." He got down off the wagon, took hold of Prince's bridle, and led him around the hole in the road. The horse pulled back, but Enoch's calm voice quieted the animal, and before long the family was trekking back to their house.

With Thunder sniffing by their side, Enoch and Tom inspected the structure. At first they were unable to open the front door. "The house is unsettled. The earthquake shook it askew a bit," Enoch said, using a lever to lift the door into place. Thunder went to his rug on the porch, circled a few times, then plunked himself down on it.

Once inside Enoch and Tom found only minor damage. Furniture had shifted and a few dishes had fallen from a shelf and broken.

When they felt it was safe, Fiona went inside. She pointed to the shards of a mirror scattered on the floor. "A broken mirror!" She moaned. "Seven years of bad luck!"

"Of all people, you know that's foolish talk, Fiona," Enoch admonished her.

"Besides, we've had good luck," said Tom. "We're safe and there's not much damage and . . ."

"And we're alive—and together," Fiona added with a grateful smile.

"We'll be safe here," Enoch said to Fiona. "Why don't you lie down for a while? Tom and I will go down the hill to the flakes and find out how bad the damage is, and see if anyone needs help."

"I'll just clean up a bit first, then I'll lie down." Fiona pointed to the broken mirror. "Don't let Thunder in until I've swept up all the splinters."

Suddenly the earth shuddered again and Fiona raced into Enoch's arms. "Oh, God, please be with us," she cried, burying her face in Enoch's chest.

"He is with us, my girl," Enoch said tenderly. "He is with us."

Tom ran to the porch and threw his arms around Thunder, who was trembling. "It'll be all right, boy," he whispered.

Enoch came to the door with Fiona. "That was just a small aftershock, see? Things will quiet down soon. I think each one will be less than the one before." He put his arm around Fiona. "Do you want us to stay until they're over?"

"No, you need to see how the others have fared." She kissed her husband. "See? I'm fine now. You go."

Tom, Thunder, and Enoch headed down to the

lower road and stages. As they descended they could see the flakes were shattered, and half of the shack where the women cleaned the fish had fallen clear down onto the beach.

Tom gasped when he saw the harbor. "The water . . . It's gone!"

The entire seabed of Rumble Reach was visible. Fish flailed against the rocky bottom. Water rats scampered into holes, and birds that had surged into the sky when the land shook now dropped onto the branches of uprooted trees.

"The earthquake shook the water out of the harbor," Enoch explained. "It's like tipping a bowl of soup and spilling it out of the dish."

"But where did it all go?" Tom wondered.

"Be careful, Tom," Enoch said as they cautiously climbed over the tangled cod nets and the broken limbs and branches that had been the stages, to get to the dry seabed.

Bert, Eddie, Nancy, and Ruby were already there, along with other folks from the island, carrying pails and filling them with the floundering fish. "Come on!" Bert yelled. "Come and get 'em while the takin's good!"

"We've got enough fish here for a big chowder!" Ruby called.

"Ten big chowders!" Nancy giggled as a slippery cod flipped out of her hands.

Thunder suddenly barked and leaped down the steep bank to the shore. He raced to Ruby and pulled at her apron with his teeth.

"Get away!" she screamed. "Tom! Get this animal away from me!"

Thunder let go, then turned to the children, barking, circling, and nudging at their arms and clothes.

Tom and Enoch ran over the mucky sand and rocks. "Come, Thunder," Enoch yelled. Thunder raced to Enoch and Tom, barking at them frantically. Then back again he flew to Ruby and the children.

Ruby screamed. "Amos! The dog's gone mad!"

Amos appeared on the edge of the shattered, teetering dock. "Get that animal away from my children!" He disappeared into what remained of the fish hut.

But Thunder kept circling, herding the group closer to the shoreline.

Amos emerged from the hut carrying a rifle. "Get out of the way, Ruby," he yelled as he took aim.

Crack! With a yelp Thunder fell to the ground!

"   **N**o!" Tom screamed, leaping over the rubble and racing to Thunder.

"The dog is mad!" Amos growled, still aiming the rifle at the dog.

"Amos, you fool! Put that gun down!" Enoch yelled. "You could kill the children!"

Amos dropped the gun to his side. "I killed that evil hound, anyway."

"*You're* the evil hound, you . . . you pelt of a tripe!" Tom screamed at Amos as he dashed to his dog.

Thunder, who was bleeding from the shoulder, struggled to stand. Tom tried to lift him, but he was too heavy. "Help me, Enoch!" Tom, looking back over his shoulder, gasped. "Oh-me-cod-oh-me-cod! Thunder was warnin' us!

Look!" He pointed to the ocean beyond Eastern Head. A wall of water as high as the cliffs was roaring toward Rumble Reach. The monstrous wave soared so high it blocked out the late afternoon sun.

"Tidal wave!" Fiona screamed from the edge of the upper road. "Get out! Quick!"

Amos dropped the rifle and scrambled to Ruby and the children. They ran over the wet stones, slipping and falling. "Hurry!" Ruby shrieked as they raced for the hillside. Other men, women, and children on the beach stumbled in panic toward the shore. "The hill! Get up the hill!" came the call. Women tugged little ones from off the slimy beach rocks and the children screamed and bawled in fright.

"Oh, God in Heaven, protect us. Save us, save us!" The sounds of praying voices faded in the roar of the oncoming wave.

Tom tried again to drag Thunder, but the dog yelped in pain. "I won't leave you, Thunder," Tom said, tears streaming down his cheeks.

The sound of the rushing water was overpowering as the mountainous wave came closer, rising higher and higher as it squeezed between the narrows.

"Run, Tom!" Fiona called hysterically. "Leave the dog and get out!"

Enoch suddenly appeared at Tom's side. "I've got him, son." He boosted the heavy dog over his shoulders. "Now run, boy! Run for your life!"

Tom ran with Enoch, not wanting to desert him, as they slipped over the rocky terrain and up the hillside. When Tom looked behind him, the water was gushing like a colossal waterfall into the seabed of Rumble Reach. The tidal wave created great winds that knocked them to their knees and blew dirt into their eyes.

"We've got to get up higher," Enoch yelled, gasping for breath.

Ken Rideout raced toward them and shouted over the roar of the sea. "I'll take 'im for a spell!" He pulled Thunder from Enoch and hoisted him onto his own back. "Keep movin'! Don't look back!"

Just as they reached the top of the hill, the tidal wave swept in with all its fury, crashing over the beach, the houses, the trees. The crest of the giant wave lifted houses and boats from the shore and smashed them onto the sides of the hill where the flakes had been.

The sounds of shattering wood and the roaring wave were deafening as people raced to the front of Enoch's house, watching the scene in horror. Ruby, holding Nancy's hand, stood sobbing at the sight below. Amos and Bert stared as if in a trance. Ken put Thunder down gently, then flung his arm around Eddie. He patted his son's back comfortingly while Rowena, in her mother's arms, buried her face against the wind and the thunderous sound of water.

As fast as it had come, the water subsided and rolled back to the narrows once more, gathering itself together and squeezing out to the sea. For a second time the harbor was empty except for the stages, the shacks, and the bridge to the mainland, all of which were broken like broom straws on the dry seabed.

Suddenly the ground shivered and rocks and gravel skittered down the hillside. "It's the end of the world!" Ruby screamed.

"Stop it, Ruby," Margaret scolded. "The children are frightened enough!" She kissed Rowena, who was crying uncontrollably. "Hush, it's not the end of the world, my child," she said soothingly. "It's an earthquake and it will stop soon."

"That was just an aftershock, my girl," Enoch explained. "We may well have more."

"Where's Thunder?" Rowena blubbered. "Is he dead?"

"No. Thunder will be all right," Margaret comforted her.

Tom stayed on the ground, his arms around Thunder.

Fiona bent down and inspected Thunder's wound. "We'll get him to a doctor as soon as things quiet down."

"How?" Tom cried, getting up. "The bridge is gone! And the boats are all busted up!"

Thunder lay still as Margaret examined the blood-matted fur on the dog's back. "It looks like the bullet just grazed him; there's no bullet hole." She stood up and put her arm around Tom. "I'll take care of Thunder, Tom. Don't you worry. He may be a bit sore for a while, but I'll fix him up just fine." She patted the dog's head. "You wise, clever dog." Thunder's tail wagged slowly.

"He was tryin' to warn us, Pa," Bert said accusingly to his father.

"Never mind the dog now," Amos said gruffly. Then he yelled, "There's another wave comin' into the harbor!"

Ruby gasped. "Not again!"

Fiona leaned into Enoch's arms as they turned to see the oncoming danger. Tom knelt with one arm around Thunder and said a silent prayer as the rumble of water grew louder. Rowena put her hands over her ears and screamed. They watched in awe as the ocean wall pressed through the narrow gap between Back o' the Moon and the mainland. The mountain of water swelled, then tumbled into the dry bed of the harbor with a roar. Again the monstrous wave lifted the boats and houses that had been left stranded and broken on the waterless inlet. With the echoing crash of breaking glass and ripping wood, the wave heaved the wreckage onto the shore.

The water receded more slowly this time, dragging with it the debris it had left scattered and destroyed. And this time, the harbor stayed filled, but overflowing with rubble.

"Our house!" Nancy cried out. "The wave took it this time!" The square green house bobbed in the waves like a toy, its roof and top story still visible.

"By great Neptune's tongue!" Amos yelled. "Every bloody thing we own is gone!"

"What'll we do? Where will we live?" Ruby moaned.

Tom saw Enoch give a questioning look to Fiona, who nodded back to him.

"You and your family can stay with us for now," Enoch offered.

Tom clutched at Fiona's arm. Surely Amos wasn't being invited to stay with them! Not after shooting Thunder!

By the time night arrived, the waters in the harbor had gone back to their normal level, and the ground tremors were slight and came far apart. It was time to make decisions for shelter. Amos and Bert were to stay with the Murrays. The Rideouts' porch had broken off the main house, but otherwise they found only minor damage inside, so Nancy and Ruby were to move in with them. People who lived down by the bridge and had lost their homes, quickly fashioned tilts—lean-tos of wood scraps and canvas—to shelter themselves for the night, and built campfires to keep themselves warm.

"Our boat is gone," Enoch groaned. "How can I make a livin' without a boat?"

"Perhaps we'll need to work for a fishin' establishment somewhere," Amos said.

"Never!" Enoch said. "I've been independent all my life!" He looked at Fiona, whose lips were trembling. "Now, my girl, we'll be all right. We still have our home and enough food to get us through for a while."

"We have a baby comin' in the spring," she said with a sob.

"We'll hang on. And we do have each other," he reminded her. Tom had never seen Enoch look so distraught and haggard.

"We can always shoot game birds," Amos said. "And moose."

"You should be good at that," Tom spat out, "after shootin' my dog!"

"Shut up, you prate-box!" Bert bellowed. "Don't you talk to my pa like that!"

"You chucklehead!" Tom screamed back at him. "If I had a face like yours, I'd walk backward!"

"Mind your mouths, both o' ya!" Fiona snapped. "We've had enough hateful talk."

"Stop all this cross-'acklin! We've got us important things to be thinkin' about, like survivin' the winter ahead!" Enoch said sharply.

Tom bit his lip. Fiona and Enoch had never yelled at him like this before. A surge of fear overcame him. The Murrays had lost everything. Now, with winter coming and a new baby on the way, he'd be one added burden. He'd only made things worse by yappin' at Amos and Bert. No wonder Enoch and Fiona were right mad at him. Maybe now they'd send him back to the mission!

He couldn't bear the thought of leaving Fiona and Enoch, but hadn't he known that it was all too good to be true? They had opened their home to him, but had they really opened their hearts?

If Tom were sent away, what would happen to Thunder? Tom would probably never see him again!

the nights were cold in late November, and the supplies of coal on the island were dwindling. Women collected scraps of wood and kept the stoves burning. The men chopped up what was left of stages and houses too damaged to repair. They piled the wood by the two remaining island houses—the Rideouts' and the Murrays'. The other houses, built close to the shore, were destroyed.

Most folks from Back o' the Moon Island whose homes had been demolished decided to take what belongings they had left and cross over to the mainland in a rescue boat. They hoped to find shelter with friends or relatives in Chance-Along. The boat would come back periodically for more passengers.

That first evening after the quake, Fiona boiled up fish from the buckets and made chowder with onions, potatoes, and canned milk. The Rideouts and the Bosworths crowded around the Murrays' kitchen as Enoch said grace. "We thank you, Lord, for our families, for our friends, and for the provisions you've given us."

"And for Tom and Thunder, who've enriched our lives," Fiona added.

"Don't know what we would've done without 'em," Ken Rideout agreed.

Tom swallowed hard as he felt tears welling up. *See?* he told himself. *Fiona still wants me, despite my blat mouthin' Amos and Bert.* He hoped Enoch wasn't still mad.

"Oh, my!" Enoch quipped, as Fiona spooned out the chowder into bowls. "This is a fine kettle of fish we're in!" Everyone, including Amos, laughed.

"Yes, our lives were all spared, thanks to that dog!" Ruby gestured to Thunder, who was curled on his rug near the stove. She gave a meaningful look to Amos, who concentrated on his soup.

"I hope Thunder will be all right," Tom said.

"He was tryin' so hard to tell us the earthquake and the tidal wave were comin'."

"Thunder will be all right," Margaret assured him. "After supper I'll clean the wound and bandage it." Thunder seemed to understand and thumped his tail.

Margaret brought bread pudding with currants, that she had made the day before, and after a brisk cup of tea, life seemed almost normal again.

Before Margaret went home, she tended to Thunder, who whined as she cleaned and poured antiseptic on his wound, then bandaged his shoulder. "He never even tried to nip at me," she said. "He knew I was tryin' to help him." She put her arm around Tom as she left. "I'll be over tomorrow to change his dressing."

Thunder curled up and put his head between his paws. His big brown eyes closed and he fell asleep.

Later, as Tom went up the stairs to his room, he asked Enoch, "What if we have another quake? Will the house cave in?"

"I think the worst is over now," Enoch told him.

"Just the same, I'm glad I'm sleepin' down here in the parlor," said Bert.

Enoch stuffed more wood into the stove and Fiona made the couches up with sheets and blankets.

"We'll be fine. Good night," said Amos. Then he added, "And . . . thank you."

Tom couldn't sleep. He wished he had his grandfather's watch with its comforting *ticktock*. But even his pocket watch wouldn't be able to drown out the terrifying images of the earthquake. With his eyes shut he could still see the great wall of black water bursting through the narrows and carrying his world away. He thought of Thunder, and how the dog had stood in front of Prince, keeping them at a safe distance from the belfry of the church when it fell. His wonderful dog. Now Thunder was in pain and hurt—all because of that Amos Bosworth.

Amos was sleeping in the room next to Thunder! Tom rolled and tossed in his bed. Surely Amos must realize by now that Thunder saved the whole town. But still . . .

Tom decided to stay with Thunder all night. He grabbed his pillow and blanket, then treaded softly down the stairs. In the parlor Amos was snoring loudly. Bert had a pillow over his head and his arm flung over the edge of the couch.

Tom tiptoed into the kitchen. In the glow of the wood stove, he saw Thunder look up and wag his tail slowly. "I'm stayin' with you," he told the dog. "Just in case." Tom placed the pillow on the floor and pulled the blanket around him. To the rhythm of Thunder's soft snores, Tom soon fell into a fitful sleep.

Outside the window the northern lights were flickering in the sky when Tom heard footsteps. Someone was standing in the doorway to the kitchen. Amos! What was he doing?

Tom waited silently, certain that Amos hadn't seen him in the corner. Amos picked up a log from the pile near the stove. Tom made ready to spring up and tackle him, when Amos opened the stove and heaved the wood into the embers. Tom didn't move, trying not to breathe.

Once the log began to spark and burn, Amos

closed the stove and walked over to Thunder. He bent down. "Good boy," he whispered, patting Thunder's head. "I'm right sorry."

Thunder's tail thumped a few times in response. Tom watched through half-closed eyes as Amos once again patted Thunder and then went back to the couch in the parlor.

Soon Tom could hear Amos's even breathing. Had Tom been dreaming? Amos had sounded truly remorseful that he had shot Thunder.

Tom closed his eyes and was almost asleep when he felt the earth shake again. He sat up, trembling. This time it was only a small rumble, as if the series of earthquakes had reached a finale and the little island had finally won its struggle for existence.

At the Murrays' dinner table the second night, the conversation was mostly about the visit from a mainland ship. Since there were no docks left, a dinghy from the steamer came in to shore to share all the news about the mainland and to see what help was needed.

"I heard tell that the earthquake was felt as far south as Delaware in the States," Enoch said.

"According to the captain of the steamer, Chance-Along had substantial damage too," Fiona added.

"But the good news is that my brother and his family made out all right in Chance-Along," Amos said, gulping down the chicken stew Fiona had made.

"That *is* good news," said Ruby, "because we're

takin' the steamer tomorrow. We'll stay with your brother and his family, at least for now. He has a nice apartment over his store."

"What are you sayin' woman?" Amos asked with a frown.

"I'm sayin' that we're goin' to Chance-Along. We can't stay here." She glared at her husband. "We have no house, or have you forgotten?"

"Well, maybe we can stay at my brother's place . . . but just for the winter," Amos mumbled.

"It'll be fun to live in Chance-Along," Nancy said. "I could even go to school there. I could learn to read real books and . . . Oh, it would be right wonderful! I could go places . . . anywhere."

"What do ya mean 'go places'?" Bert snickered. "Where ya gonna go?"

Nancy crossed her arms. "When you read you can go anywhere . . . in the stories, you chucklehead!"

"We'll be busy enough without you spendin' all your time readin' books," Ruby scolded.

Bert snickered. "Besides, you'd be tired of school in a week!"

Nancy scowled at her brother. "Would not!"

"We don't know if there's a school left standin'" over there," Amos interrupted. "So why argue about it?"

"Tomorrow we'll move to Chance-Along for the winter, see," Ruby declared. "We're not imposin' on the Murrays another day. We're leavin'!" She shook a finger at Amos. "And not another word about it!"

Tom saw Fiona exchange glances with Enoch and the shadow of a smile pass between them. Tom wanted to cheer that Amos and his family would be leaving, although he was convinced that Amos was truly sorry he had hurt Thunder. In fact, Tom had seen Amos even take scraps of meat from his own plate—food that was now scarce— and feed it to Thunder when he thought no one was looking.

"We'll come back in the spring and rebuild," Amos insisted. "My father and grandfather home-steaded on our land, and you can bet your miser-able life I'm not about to give it up."

"And just where do we get the money to rebuild?" Ruby asked.

"The people on the rescue boat said the government's sendin' along aid for those who lost their homes," Enoch told them.

"They're takin' collections in churches and schools all over Newfoundland," Fiona said.

"I'll believe it when I see the money in my hand, maid," Amos grumbled. "But I'll find a way to rebuild. You'll see."

"If we do, it won't be that close to the water, let me tell," Ruby sputtered. "We've had storms before that nearly washed us out. They should have been warning enough."

After dinner Margaret and Ken Rideout came over. "We put Rowena to bed and Eddie's watchin' her," Ken told them.

Margaret tended Thunder's wound. "Good boy," she murmured, gently removing the bandage.

Tom couldn't bring himself to look at the ugly red slash on Thunder's shoulder.

"How's the dog doin'?" Amos asked Margaret.

"The lesion is fillin' in nicely." Thunder lay quietly, as if knowing that Margaret was trying to help him. She dabbed the gash with something from a bottle and Thunder whined.

"Poor thing," Fiona said. "He's suffered with that bullet wound more than he lets on."

"That gun's big enough to bring down a bull moose," Ken Rideout said.

"It's only by the grace of God that Thunder's alive," Ruby added.

"Well, you were the one screamin' for help," Amos defended himself. "I thought he'd gone mad!"

"You wouldn't harm Thunder again, now would you, Amos?" Ken's question was more like a warning.

Amos stood up. "Of course not! I'd sooner shoot myself than lay a hand on that dog!" he exclaimed angrily. "He saved our lives. Now let's not talk about it ever again."

"Yes, enough said," Enoch agreed.

The next morning Tom and the Murrays, along with the Rideouts, helped the Bosworths get their belongings onto the rescue ship out in the harbor. Thunder followed Tom down to the dinghy, limping slowly.

"Look at all that ballicatter!" Enoch pointed to

the glittering frozen spray that had gathered on the shoreline.

"We'll soon be iced in," Ken said.

"Once the ice is safe, we'll cross over and visit," Margaret said to Ruby.

Ruby hugged Margaret and then Fiona. "We'll come back as often as we can. Don't have that baby until spring, when we're all together again." She planted a kiss on Fiona's cheek, then climbed into the dinghy.

"The baby's due in April," Fiona reminded her.

Nancy kissed Rowena, who started to cry. "Now, none o' that," Nancy scolded, but her eyes had filled with tears too.

"You're a good beast," Amos said softly as he bent over Thunder. "I'm owin' to ya."

Bert petted Thunder's head. "Good-bye, boy. Thank you for savin' us." He looked up at Tom and gave a half smile. "'Bye, Tom."

Tom nodded. "'Bye," he said.

"Don't get in any trouble over there," Eddie teased Bert.

"I'll stay as pure as the driven snow," Bert said, "until you come over to make a ruckus."

The Bosworths stood at the rail as the rescue ship left the harbor. The Murrays and Rideouts waved until the boat became a small object in the distance.

"Now there's no one on Back o' the Moon, 'cept us," Tom noted. "Everyone else has deserted the island."

"And here I am with a baby comin'," Fiona said. "I'm not sure we should stay, Enoch."

"We'll be all right," Enoch said. "We ain't screedless, you know, maid."

"You're right. We ain't lost *everything*. We got our house and each other, and enough wood to last us through the worst of the winter."

"Once the ice is in, in another month or so, we can cross over to Chance-Along for provisions," Ken said.

Fiona smiled. "We'll just snuggle in and settle down for now."

"And who knows," Margaret added, taking Rowena by the hand, "this may be a whole new adventure for all of us." She ruffled Thunder's ears. "Right, boy?"

Thunder whined and thumped his tail.

By early December winter had set in fast. It was quiet on the nearly deserted island. The deep snowdrifts muffled sounds, except for the whistling of the wind through the trees.

Enoch and Tom brought in the hay from the outer pasture. Ken Rideout had a barn, so Prince would winter there. The men piled the hay against the inside walls of the shed. Then they brought Prince in from the outer pasture barn. "There should be enough hay here for one horse for the winter," Enoch told Ken. "And we have plenty of oats from that last trip you took to Chance-Along."

"I'll come get it tomorrow," Ken said.

"Once the ice is thick, can't Prince take us by sleigh over the harbor to Chance-Along?" Tom asked.

"If the bridge was in, I'd take the sleigh, but the ice on the harbor is slippery, and the snow drifts leave bare spots," Enoch said.

"Dogs do better on the ice," Ken said. "Horses can slip and break a leg."

"When Thunder's wound is healed up we'll give him a try with a slide," Enoch said. "But for now I don't like to put a strain on his shoulder with the harness." Tom must have looked worried, because Enoch patted his back. "Don't worry, lad. We have plenty of food and rations. We don't need to make Thunder work for now."

Enoch, Tom, Ken, and Eddie pulled broken nets in from along the shore. They spent long hours repairing and scunning them together with twine and hooks and linnet oil, while curtains of snow crept up the windowpanes. In the frigid afternoons, Tom gave reading lessons to Eddie, who wanted to surprise his folks at Christmastime. "When I start reading from the Bible all by myself . . . well, that will be the biggest surprise and best present ever," Eddie said.

Tom also helped Enoch to make a cradle for

the baby, fitting together pieces of maple that had been sanded to a smooth gloss. Fiona hugged and kissed them both when they presented her with the exquisite little bed.

It seemed Fiona was always busy knitting blankets, buntings, and sweaters for the baby. She'd hold up the finished project and say, "Isn't it sweet?" Then she'd kiss it and put it in the cradle with all the other baby things she'd made or collected.

Thunder stayed in the house most of the time, sleeping by the fire, or sitting by Tom, his head leaning against the boy's lap. "Thunder, you're droolin' all over me," Tom said. "You need a bib!" The next morning Fiona took a piece of flour bag and made a bib for Thunder. "Isn't it sweet?" she asked. Everyone laughed when she tied it around the dog's thick neck.

At night Fiona and Enoch sat in the lamp-light and told Tom legends of old Newfoundland, of pirates and ghosts that supposedly haunted their island country. Ken and Margaret often came over with Eddie and Rowena and added more stories.

One of Tom's favorites was the story of Captain Kidd and the treasure of gold that he concealed on the island of Newfoundland. "Do you suppose it's still there?" Tom asked.

"Maybe we'll go and search for ourselves someday," Eddie said. "Would ya like to do that, Tom?"

"Aye! We'd bring back a boatload of gold and . . . build a castle here at Back o' the Moon!" Tom answered.

"Oh, be careful, me boys!" Enoch warned. "You'll need to watch out for the ghost."

"Aye," Ken piped up. "There's a ghost guardin' that treasure."

"Stop it right now," Margaret said, putting her hands over Rowena's ears. "You'll frighten the little one."

"I wants to hear the story!" Rowena screamed, pushing her mother away.

"No scary stories for the likes of you," Margaret said to Rowena. "The old hag will come and give you nightmares."

"*Now* who's scarin' her?" Ken asked. "Old hag indeed!"

Margaret ignored him. "Come on, Fiona, let's fire up the kettle." They went into the kitchen, pulling Rowena along, and closed the parlor door behind them.

"Tell us about the ghosts!" Tom and Eddie begged.

Enoch continued in a low, scary voice. "Well, as true as I'm alive, there's a ghost watchin' over that treasure. Why d'ya suppose it's never been found?"

"When the treasure was hidden, one pirate was chosen to guard the gold forever," Ken told them.

"I don't think we should tell the boys . . . about all this." Enoch looked at Ken questioningly, then winked.

"You're right, boy," Ken agreed. "It might scarify 'em to death."

"Tell us!" Tom and Eddie yelled together.

"Well, first off *this* is what became of the pirate who was chosen to guard the treasure." Ken made a sweeping slash across his neck with his finger. Then he crossed his eyes and stuck out his tongue.

"They killed him?" Tom asked.

"Their own crewmate?" Eddie's eyes were huge.

"Aye! That's how the gold is guarded forever. The ghost stays with the treasure . . . wherever Capt'n Kidd planted it."

"We wouldn't be ascared of any ol' ghosts, would we, Tom?" Eddie said.

"N'arn! There ain't no such thing as ghosts," Tom agreed. "But where did Capt'n Kidd plant the treasure anyways?"

"I hears tell it might be at Cape Race," Enoch said. "Or on Signal Hill in St. John's."

"I've heard Cape Spear or Freshwater Bay," Ken joined in.

"But—and this is the best part—on stormy nights when the wind is right, you can hear the *hollies*, the ghost cries of the pirate who's guardin' the treasure"—Enoch lowered his voice and motioned the boys closer—"right here in Back o' the Moon!"

Both boys gasped and their mouths dropped open.

"'Tis the gospel truth," Ken whispered. "Listen when the wind is blowin' and you'll hear the hollies."

"Good morrow to you! I don't believe a word," Tom said, but his voice trembled.

"That's all pishogue," Eddie said. "Ain't it?"

At that moment a piercing whistle came from the kitchen. The boys jumped and Thunder, who'd been sitting by the stove, leaped up with a bark. Enoch and Ken doubled over, laughing.

It was only the kettle!

After tea and bakeapple tarts, the Rideouts went out into the dark night. Eddie turned before leaving and said, "There ain't no such thing as ghosts, right, Tom?"

"It's foolish blather," Tom answered. "That's all it is."

During these winter evenings, Fiona sat listening to the stories while her knitting needles clicked and clicked and the fire snapped and hissed.

As her belly swelled, Fiona took to wearing bungalows—loose-fitting clothes—including old flannel shirts of Enoch's. "He must be a little roly-poly," Enoch often said, patting Fiona's tummy.

"He? And what if it's a little girl?" Fiona would respond.

"Well, if so our wee maid is a roly-poly, like her mother!" was Enoch's teasing answer. Then he'd duck as Fiona threw a pillow at him.

Tom wondered if Enoch and Fiona hoped the baby would be a boy. And if so, would they still want him . . . or need him? This was a foolish thought. Tom chided himself. Of course Enoch and Fiona would still want him. Hadn't they said so a dozen times?

Besides, a little boy would be right wonderful! Tom could teach him to play ball and to fish. Still, Tom wasn't Enoch and Fiona's true son. And the baby wouldn't be his true brother or sister, either.

On one of these nights, Tom pressed his face into the white lightning streak on Thunder's chest. "Fiona and Enoch will still need us when the baby comes, you know," he told the dog. "And the baby will need us too. Sure they will. So don't you worry, boy. We'll be okay, Thunder, just as long as we stick together."

Christmas was coming and Tom recalled the holiday festivities at the mission when everyone gathered around the tree and sang carols. There were presents, too. Not one child went without a gift.

Tom wondered what he should give to Fiona and Enoch. He couldn't get to the stores at Chance-Along, and even if he could, he had no money. So Tom was relieved when Enoch said, "Tom, we won't be celebrating Christmas the way you're probably used to celebrating. Don't worry about gettin' anything for Fiona and me. We keep Christmas simple—without all the fuss. After all, Jesus was born in a barn to a humble family."

Fiona added, "We don't have much to give this year in the way of gifts. We've lost so much with the earthquake and the tidal wave. But we do have each other and that is the best gift of all."

On Christmas day Fiona handed Tom a small white box tied with a gold ribbon. Tom was alarmed. They were giving him a gift and he had nothing to give them! "Oh, but you said—"

Fiona quickly interrupted. "This isn't really a Christmas present, Tom. We would have given it to you anyway. It belongs to you."

Tom opened the box and gasped. "Grandfather's pocket watch!" The gold watch gleamed. It had been polished to a bright shine and the engraved Celtic knot stood out clearly. Tom popped it open. The broken crystal had been replaced. Even the face and hands looked like new. Tom put the watch to his ear and heard its familiar ticking. His eyes filled with tears.

"We knew it meant a lot to you, so we took it to the jeweler at Chance-Along the day we went to Dr. Sullivan's," Enoch explained.

"Ken picked it up one day when he was able to get over to the mainland," Fiona said.

Tom threw his arms around Fiona and then Enoch. "Thank you," he whispered. "Thank you so much."

Later, after dinner, they were about to have dessert—hot fig duff, a boiled flour pudding with raisins—when they heard a banging on the door.

"I'll go," Tom said, expecting to see one of the Rideouts. Thunder barked and followed him.

Six strange creatures—one with the head of a horse, another with a crown, and all with ghostly masks—stood on the threshold.

tom gaped at the strange sight. What was going on? Muffled laughs came from under the masks. "Any mummers 'loud in?" they asked.

"We're nice mummers. We're good jannies," said the horse in a hollow voice. "We're comin' in to dance with ya!" The group stomped the snow from their feet, pushed past Tom, and crowded into the house.

"Who are you?" Tom asked.

"Don't ask," whispered one of the mummers, who wore a kitchen pot for a hat and red yarn for a beard. "It's against the rules."

Tom recalled that if you guessed who was under the mask, they would have to reveal themselves, and no mummer wanted that.

They had to be the Rideouts! After all, there

were no other families on the island. But there were only four Rideouts, and none of them was the right size—no jannie here was small like Rowena, nor thin like Ken, nor chubby like Margaret. Who were they? Where did they come from? How did they get here?

Enoch and Fiona came into the kitchen and looked in astonishment at the six creatures. Two of the mummers began speaking to each other in high-pitched jannie talk.

"Nowwho'sdatscraggyladmedear?" one sang out.

"'E'sdaonedatamoswantstowarnboutdedog," another mummer answered in a chirping voice.

"What are they sayin'?" Tom was bewildered.

"I've no idea," Fiona answered.

"And what has this to do with Christmas?"

"Not a thing that I can see," Enoch whispered.

The mummer with the golden crown didn't say a word. But another mummer, who wore a stringy mop as a wig, danced a jig and sang, "We're here, my dears, to entertain you!" Tom couldn't tell if it was a man or woman—it wore a patchwork skirt topped with a man's shirt and a yellow-and-black necktie on backward. Its feet were huge, and as the creature danced, Tom could see red-striped stockings that went up to its knees. "Let me introduce myself," the stranger said with a bow. My name is Pickle Herring. And I am the Mischief Maker."

The jannie with the horse's head said in an echoing voice, "I am the Horsy-hops!" He pulled a string and the horse's mouth opened and shut with a knocking sound. Tom could see nails for the horse's teeth.

The Horsy-hops pointed to the stranger with the crown. "This here's the Fool. And your dog knows this to be true."

The Fool nodded.

Thunder stood by the parlor door and watched, his head tilted quizzically.

Pickle Herring and Fool? What could that mean? Tom glanced at Fiona and Enoch, who were laughing and shaking their heads.

A mummer played a harmonica through a hole in his yellow papier-mâché mask. The Fool stood by silently while the other mummers danced and stomped their feet on the linoleum floor. Pickle Herring pulled Fiona by the hand

and she, in turn, pulled Enoch. All eight danced in a circle. "Come on, Tom," said Fiona. "These circle dances stand for the different cycles of life." But Tom shook his head. He didn't feel at ease joining in with these strange creatures.

When they stopped, a jannie with a lunker—a yellow oilskin hat—and a beard of pine needles glued to his pillowslip mask, croaked, "Now it's time for you to give us a grog or some of that duff pudding I spy on the table."

"Why, certainly," said Fiona, scooping pudding into dishes while Enoch filled mugs with hot cider. The mummers sat on the floor by Thunder and gobbled up their treats through the mouth holes in their masks. Never once did they lift their masks.

Thunder sniffed at the strange costumes and the jannies spoke to him in their squeaky jannie talk. "Whadafine'ncleverbeastiewe'ave'ere."

"An'eblongsright'erewiddatbye."

"Now, this here dog is the reason for our visit," Pickle Herring finally said. He took the crown from the Fool and placed it on the dog's head. "I hereby crown you the King of Dogdom," he proclaimed. Thunder cocked his head and the crown slipped over one ear.

Everyone laughed.

"You are the finest animal on this great island of Newfoundland. And this here's the greatest fool," Pickle Herring said, pointing to the silent mummer.

Surprisingly, the Fool turned to Tom and spoke in a guttural whisper. "Now hear to my warnin', me boy. Don't risk your dog by bringin' him to Chance-Along. Keep him here at Back o' the Moon. There's peril waitin' across the bay."

The odd group then got up, went to the door, bowed, waved good-bye with their hats, and left.

"Who were they?" Fiona asked. "I couldn't tell."

"One of them reminded me of someone, but I can't put my finger on it," Enoch said. "They must have come across from Chance-Along. The ice is strong enough now."

"They came to pay homage to Thunder," Fiona said, "the King of Dogdom!"

"No," Tom said. "They came to warn me . . . and Thunder. There's some sort of danger waitin' for us in Chance-Along."

Fiona and Enoch looked at each other, then Fiona said, "It's too bad their visit had to end with the Fool's warning."

"Don't worry about it, Tom," Enoch said, after thinking about it for a moment. "After all, the message came from 'the Fool.' You can't rely on anything a fool tells you."

But when Tom went to bed that night, even the soothing, familiar *ticktock* beneath his pillow couldn't drown out the Fool's throaty warning: *There's peril waitin' across the bay.*

During January, blizzards drove the snow in drifts so high that the windows were completely covered. Enoch and Tom shoveled and threw ashes onto the slippery walkways. Fiona stayed in the house, except for the times she went to see Margaret for a granny visit. Then Tom or Enoch went with her to help her walk on the icy paths. Everything seemed to be going well with Fiona and her baby.

Thunder's gunshot wound had healed nicely too, so he was let outside to play. Thunder loved to burrow his nose in the clean snow. Then he'd roll around in it like a puppy.

"We need more firewood," Enoch said one morning. "We've used more than I expected, and the pile in the woodshed is gettin' low.

Come on, Thunder. It's time to put you to work!"

Thunder stood quietly, though, as Tom hitched the harness tackle to the slide—a sled that had wide runners, like skis, to enable it to slip easily across the snow. Enoch tied a piece of canvas to a make-shift wooden mast that was hitched to the slide by a bracket. "The canvas acts like a sail and will lighten Thunder's load on the way back," he explained to Tom.

It was a sunny day with a bright blue sky and glittering snow. Tom and Enoch wore heavy woolen jackets, hats, gloves, and masks to protect themselves from the cold. "Thunder will have enough to carry on the return," Enoch said, so neither of them climbed aboard the slide but walked alongside.

Thunder jogged merrily on the harbor ice, sniffing the breeze and looking back now and then to make sure Tom and Enoch were catching up.

"He's as happy as a clam in a mudflat to be outside again," Tom said.

Once they approached Eastern Head, they could see beyond the ice to the sapphire blue ocean with its white spray of breaking waves. The woods in back of Eastern Head were loaded with trees, whereas the shoreline near their home only had small, scrubby saplings, so each fall Enoch came out to Eastern Head to cut timber. Now he and Tom would take the rest of the wood that had been harvested and piled last year, but they would leave this year's stock of timber to dry for next winter's fires.

Thunder waited patiently as Tom and Enoch filled the slide with logs, set the sail, and headed back to the house. Thunder tugged at the slide. Once the sail filled with wind he trotted at a good clip with Enoch and Tom pacing alongside.

It was a pretty sight—Thunder's black form against the sparkling white snow, and the sail billowing above the sled. The only sounds were the flapping of the sail and swish of the runners on the snowy surface.

"Thunder's doing really well," Enoch called out. "We'll take him across to Chance-Along for supplies in a few days. Should only take an hour or so to get there if we head toward Dr. Sullivan's place. That's the nearest jut-out from the mainland."

Tom stopped. Go to Chance-Along? After the

mummer's Fool had given him that warning? Perhaps he'd say he was sick and stay home with Fiona. Still, Thunder would have to go, and that's who the warning was intended for in the first place. *Keep your dog at Back o' the Moon.*

Enoch looked over his shoulder. "You all right, Tom?" he called.

Tom ran to catch up. Should he tell Enoch his fears? Enoch and Fiona had told him not to pay a bit of attention to what the Fool had said. But still . . .

When they returned home, Tom unhitched Thunder from the slide. Thunder pawed at the kitchen door to be let in. Fiona opened the door. "Come in, my dear sweet thing," she said to the dog. "You've had a long haul." Thunder licked her hand as he scampered into the kitchen. Fiona bent down with some difficulty and wiped the wet paw prints from the linoleum with a dish rag.

"Fiona," Enoch said, frowning. "That dog should stay outside. He's trackin' mud and water all over the house. You could fall on that slippery floor."

"Very well," Fiona said. She fetched Thunder's

rug and took it out to the porch. "Come, Thunder. You can stay out here from now on." Thunder trudged out and plunked himself down on the rug. He looked up at Fiona sadly, but when she appeared with his food bowls, he stood up eagerly, his tail wagging like a flag in the wind.

Enoch and Tom put half the wood in the woodshed and stacked the rest near the back door. "I swear that dog is spoiled since he was shot," Enoch said. "He's used to bein' pampered in the house. Now he expects it, see?"

"But it's been shockin' cold outside," Tom objected. "And he was hurt pretty bad."

"Aye, but now he's well. Dogs like Thunder don't mind the cold. In fact, they love it. They're born to it—with an extra coat of fur next to their skin, like underwear!" Enoch chuckled. "They curl their tails up over their heads and stay as warm as toast."

Tom didn't answer. At least when Thunder was inside Tom knew no harm could come to him. As long as Thunder was at Back o' the Moon, there was no real danger. The peril, whatever it was, was waiting over at Chance-Along. Tom made up his mind. He'd go with Enoch to the mainland, but he wouldn't let Thunder out of his sight, not for a single moment.

Early one morning a few days later, Enoch hitched Thunder up to the slide. Then he and Tom headed out across frozen Rumble Reach, toward Chance-Along. Thunder seemed to enjoy the hike, walking briskly towing the empty slide. At times Tom and Enoch had to run to catch up with him.

They headed for the jut of land where Dr. Sullivan lived. "It's over to the east more," Enoch called, pointing. "Not directly opposite our house."

Tom squinted against the sun, but couldn't make out the distant shore distinctly. "If I had to go alone, I'd have no idea where I was heading," he told Enoch.

"You aim for that small cliff—the one that looks like a hat of woods—you know, a head with a thicket of trees for the hair. Dr. Sullivan's is a little to the right of that bluff."

Tom squinted and nodded. "Aye, that's a good marker," he said.

When they were more than halfway across the

bay, Tom could see the tall red-and-white harbor markers—the ones that warned ships of shoals—frozen solid in the ice. "Let's stop here and rest," Enoch suggested. "It won't be much farther to the other side now."

Thunder sat down, his tongue sticking out from the side of his mouth. The drool that always slipped down his chest had frozen into icicles on his white streak. "Here, let me get rid of those conkerbills," Tom said, brushing them off.

Enoch examined Thunder's paws. "He's picked up some ice. That can hurt, even bleed." Thunder yelped while Enoch pulled gently at the lumps of ice that had wedged between the dog's paw pads.

"In the spring, around March and April, when the ice becomes slush, you can't cross the bay," Enoch said. "It's too dangerous. The currents shift beneath the ice and could leave you stranded, or you could fall through and drown."

Tom shuddered at the thought of drifting out to sea on an ice pan. "I'd rather go hungry, or eat fish guts, before I'd cross in the spring."

They continued on their trek to the mainland,

and soon the small cliff became close and clear. "There's Dr. Sullivan's!" Tom called. "I can see it now." The windows in the large, sand-colored house on the hill reflected the sun. Smoke from the chimney curled through the trees. Thunder barked and began to race toward land. Soon they were pulling the slide up onto the shore.

Enoch plunked himself down on one of the boulders that lined the waterfront. Evidence of the tidal wave was everywhere. The remains of Dr. Sullivan's wharves stuck up at odd angles from beneath the snow. Broken trees reached up like bony fingers to the sky, their limbs gone. "By the great codfish! It's a blessin' that Dr. Sullivan built his house up on that hillside," Enoch said. "It was spared from the wave."

Tom sat on a log. "I have an idea," he said suddenly. "Why don't you go on ahead to Chance-Along with the slide and I'll wait here with Thunder. That will give 'im a rest."

At that moment Dr. Sullivan came out of his house and walked down to the shore. "Lo and behold you! Tom! Enoch! How's that wife of yours doin'?"

"She's as fit as a fiddle," Enoch answered. "Say,

Doc, do you mind if we leave our dog here while we go into town with the slide?"

"That'll be fine," Dr. Sullivan said. He went to Thunder and let the dog sniff his hands. "I heard how he knew the earthquake was about to happen and saved folks from the tidal wave." Dr. Sullivan sat down by Tom. "Animals have another sense, I swear. They can feel and smell danger long before it comes."

"He's a right clever dog," Enoch acknowledged. "He can pull a sledful of lumber, so we're goin' to try him out with supplies today."

The doctor picked up one of Thunder's paws. "He's got a few deep scratches from the trip over here. I'll put somethin' on them," he said. He looked up at Enoch. "Say, is it true that Amos shot this dog?"

"Amos thought the dog had gone mad, attackin' his children and other such nonsense. He should've known better," Enoch told him.

"That man's right sorry, let me tell. He's always talkin' about how this dog saved his family. He's feelin' pretty bad about all that's happened since," Dr. Sullivan said.

"What else is he sorry about?" Tom asked.

"Oh, didn't you hear? When you first got the dog, Amos was inquirin' everywhere to find who the owner might be. Well, just before Christmas he got a telegram from Gloucester, down in the States. Seems a ship's captain by the name o' Fowler lost him overboard during that August squall. He's offerin' a reward."

"No!" Tom cried out. "Thunder is *my* dog, Enoch!"

"Don't get upset, son. It might not be Thunder who he's after."

Dr. Sullivan touched Tom's arm. "Oh, what a chucklehead I am. I wasn't thinkin' how much he means to you. I figured you'd heard."

"No one told us," Enoch said. "We knew Amos had been in touch with fisheries last summer, but we didn't know he got a response."

"Seems word got out about the dog. Anyways, when the telegram arrived the news was all over town," said Dr. Sullivan. "Everyone here knows what's goin' on, especially in the telegraph office. It's always big news when someone gets a telegram."

"So the owner's from the States," said Enoch.

"Yep. From Gloucester, down in Massachusetts."

"He didn't take good care of Thunder," Tom protested. "He shouldn't be allowed to own a dog."

"Tom . . ." Enoch put his hand on Tom's shoulder, but Tom pulled away.

"This here Fowler person won't be comin' until spring," Dr. Sullivan said. "Maybe he'll disremember it by then."

"I'd go round the world for Thunder. *I'd* never disremember 'im!" Tom retorted.

"If this Mr. Fowler is the owner, there's not much we can do about it," Enoch said.

"You mean we'll have to give him back?" Tom exclaimed.

"If it were you, Tom, wouldn't you want him back?" Enoch asked softly.

Tom didn't answer. He understood what Enoch was telling him, but . . . how could he give up Thunder? He couldn't. He *wouldn't*!

"No need to worry about it now," said Dr. Sullivan. "But do be careful around Chance-Along. Most folks have neither meat nor malt. They've lost everything with the tidal wave. A reward would be mighty temptin'."

"See? We should have given heed to that mummer and his warning about Chance-Along," Tom said.

"Tom, that mummer, whoever he was, must have known about Mr. Fowler and his claim to Thunder. Well, try not to worry. We won't bring Thunder to the mainland again. Meanwhile, we don't have to deal with Mr. Fowler till spring thaw. Come on, let's do our shoppin' so we can get back home."

"I'll watch Thunder," said the doctor. "Bring him up on the porch. He'll be safe here."

Tom tied Thunder to the porch rail, but before he left, Tom whispered to the dog, "Don't go off with anyone, boy." Then he hugged Thunder so tightly the dog whined.

The main street in Chance-Along was packed with hard snow. Tom and Enoch went to the Copper Kettle first for hot chocolate and a fried codfish sandwich. But Tom wasn't hungry. Why had they come to the mainland anyway? For food? He'd sooner eat barnacles than come to this town again.

"My boy, you're all upset about Thunder, aren't you?" Enoch said. "Look, if the owner contacts us, I'll offer him money. I don't know if we can afford to buy him, but we'll do everything we can do to keep Thunder." He pointed to the sandwich. "Come on, Tom, eat up. You'll be starvin' by the time we get home."

They shopped all afternoon at the general store until the slide was full. Enoch seemed very quiet. Tom knew he was worried about money and was concerned about Thunder, too. "I've got one more errand to run before we leave," Enoch finally said. "Want to come with me?"

"No, I'll wait here with the slide."

"All right. I won't be long." Enoch pulled the slide over to an iron bench, then headed down the street.

Tom slumped onto the bench. The town was unusually quiet. The tidal wave had destroyed most of the boats that had been in the water or even pulled up near the shore. Fishermen could not work without boats, so many families had left

Chance-Along to go to bigger towns like St.
John's, the capital of Newfoundland, or Corner
Brook to work at the big lumber mills on the
Humber River. They headed off to wherever they
could make money to survive. Perhaps Enoch and
Fiona would move somewhere else too. Maybe
that would be a good thing—movin' far away
where no one could find Tom or his dog.

"Hey, Tom!"

Tom looked around. Nancy Bosworth stood
nearby, dressed in boys' breeches and an orange
plaid coat that was too small for her.

"What are you doin' here, Tom?" she asked as
she approached.

"Just gettin' supplies."

"I'm goin' to school now. I can read almost
everything." She pointed to a sign in a nearby
store window and began to read slowly. "Buy . . .
win-ter . . . deep snow . . . snowshoes—"

"I don't want to talk to you, Nancy."

"Why not?"

"I've heard about your pa findin' Thunder's
real owner."

Nancy looked down at her boots. "We're all right sorry."

"As sorry as snakes. Just go away, Nancy. I never want to see any of you Bosworths again." Tom turned away from her.

Nancy didn't move, and after a few moments Tom heard her crying softly.

"Go away! Cryin' isn't goin' to change anything. Your pa—and your brother, too—they wanted Thunder themselves, and when we wouldn't give him up they made sure they'd find the real owner, just for badness. Begone with ya!"

Nancy raced off. Tom was relieved to see Enoch coming toward him.

"I saw Amos," Enoch said.

"Aye, and I saw Nancy. I don't want to hear anything about the Bosworths," Tom said. He grabbed hold of the rope tied to the front of the slide and walked briskly away.

The slide was heavy, but Tom didn't care. He wanted to get away from Chance-Along and never come back. Enoch caught up with Tom and took the rope from him. Tom ran ahead, eager to be sure that his dog was safe.

"Thunder!" Tom called out as he approached Dr. Sullivan's house. "Thunder!"

When he didn't hear the usual happy bark, Tom ran to the porch.

Thunder wasn't there!

"Thunder's gone!" he exclaimed, running up the porch steps. "Thunder!"

The back door opened quickly, and Dr. Sullivan came out with Thunder bouncing by his side. "I told you I'd take good care of 'im, lad." The doctor pointed to the dog's huge paws. "I've made 'im some boots to protect his feet on the ice, see." Tom couldn't help but smile. Thunder's paws were wrapped with canvas and strong tape. "There's nice soft lamb's wool inside." The doctor sounded pleased with himself. Thunder picked up one paw and tugged at the boot with his teeth. "No, no, boy," Dr. Sullivan shook his finger at Thunder. "Keep your boots on!" Thunder put his paw down obediently.

"Thanks, Doc," Enoch said. "I'm sure Thunder appreciates your hard work."

"I'm not so sure he does," Dr. Sullivan said with a laugh. "But a good deed is always in order." He petted Thunder's head and the dog lapped his hand. "Slobbery dog, you are! He's a real article, ain't he?"

"He's an article all right," Tom agreed. "And we sure love 'im."

On the way home Thunder's boots slipped off several times, but Tom or Enoch stopped and pulled them back on. Thunder tried to pull them off, but Tom would tell him, "It's for your own good, Thunder!"

It was getting dark by the time they got home. Tom unhitched Thunder and removed the booties from the dog's paws. Thunder drank an entire bowl of water, sank immediately onto his rug, and closed his eyes.

Tom and Enoch brought in the groceries and supplies without saying much.

"I have a nice pot of pea soup with turnip, potatoes, and carrots, and fresh bread," Fiona said, spooning the soup into large bowls. "Now, you men sit down and dig in. Your stomachs probably think your throats have been cut!" She laughed, but neither Tom nor Enoch even smiled. Finally she said, "All right, tell me what happened at Chance-Along."

"After supper," Enoch said.

They ate in silence. Then Tom excused himself and went to his room. He left the door open so he could hear Enoch tell Fiona about the telegram.

She let out a little scream. "No! We can't lose our Thunder!"

"Maybe we can offer to buy 'im," Enoch suggested. "Although I don't know where we'd get that kind of money, 'specially now with a baby comin'."

Their voices became low and Tom could only hear a few words—*Tom, boat, fisheries, no money, no boat.*

Tom threw himself on the bed and buried his head in the pillow. He'd run away, that's what he'd do. He'd take Thunder and . . . what? Where would they go? He had no relatives or friends outside the mission. And even if he could make his way back to the mission, he couldn't keep Thunder when he got there.

Fiona knocked on the open door. "Tom? Can I come in?"

"All right," he said, his voice muffled by the pillow.

Fiona sat at the foot of Tom's bed. "Enoch told me what's happened," she said. "I'm so sorry, Tom."

Tom nodded, his face still buried in the pillow. "I hate Amos and Bert."

"They're sorry for what they did, so don't hate them. Hate is like a heavy chain to carry with you. Let go of it, my child."

Tom looked up. "The hardest part is that I *know* that Thunder's owner has a right to him. But he didn't take good enough care of him, lettin' him fall overboard and all!" Tom buried his face in his pillow again. "Now we have to give him back."

"Things have a way of workin' themselves out, my dear. The Scriptures say not to be anxious about tomorrow. Each day we'll put Thunder in God's hands and let go. Whatever happens then is God's will. He loves you and wants you to be happy. We want you to be happy too."

Tom sat up. "Fiona," he blurted out. "Will you and Enoch be able . . . to . . . keep me? I mean . . . since the earthquake . . . and the boat's gone . . . the baby comin' . . . and all."

Fiona put her arms around him. "Tom, don't you believe it yet? You're family too. We'll stick together no matter what. Things will work out." Suddenly she laughed and placed Tom's hand on her belly. "Hush, now. Wait!"

After a moment, the baby moved. Tom jumped back. "I felt it! The baby's kickin' at me!"

Fiona laughed again. "The baby's all excited. He knows his brother is here." She kissed Tom on the cheek. "Tell God your concerns in your prayers. The Scriptures say, 'Throw your burdens on Him, because He cares for you.' Then don't worry anymore." Fiona blew him another kiss and left the room.

Tom put his head on the pillow. "Thank you, Lord," he prayed. "Thank you for Fiona and Enoch . . . and the baby. Please, please let us stay together, and please, somehow let me keep Thunder."

The winter was passing by quickly, with February now behind them. The March sun was brighter and higher in the sky. On warm mornings fog enclosed the island, melting the ice along the shoreline, which would then freeze again at night. Other days were like winter returning, with icy winds and brilliant blue skies, and at night, dazzling northern lights flickering red and green in the sky. The house remained cozy, warm with its blanket of snow on the roof and sparkling icicles—ice candles—hanging from the eaves.

But March was the hungry month, when salted, dried fish and meat, along with the supply of root vegetables stored for the winter, was waning. "A more hungry March we've never seen," Enoch said. "Spring will be hard with no fishin' boat and all the damage from the tidal wave."

One clear morning, two figures plodded across the still-frozen harbor to Back o' the Moon. As they approached Enoch called out, "It's Amos! And Bert's with him."

Were they coming for Thunder? It was almost spring. Wasn't that when Mr. Fowler was to come from the States? Tom grabbed Thunder by the collar and stomped through the deep melting snow to the woodshed. Rufus, the rooster, clucked angrily from the chicken coop. "Shut up, you old crow!" Tom told him. "Don't you know me yet?"

Tom unlatched the door to the woodshed, pulled Thunder inside with him, then shut it quietly behind him.

It's kinda stupid for me to hide, Tom thought. *They'll find us sooner or later. But at least I'm not givin' Thunder up easy.* He waited, listening to the melting of the ice candles on the eaves of the roof.

After several minutes he opened the door a crack and peeked outside. No one was about. Perhaps they were all in the house. He shut the door again and sat on a log. Thunder whined and pushed at the door with his paw. "No, Thunder,"

Tom whispered. "We've got to stay here." Thunder wagged his tail, then settled down on the dirt floor.

Tom closed his eyes. *Please don't let them take Thunder.*

After what seemed like an hour, and sore from sitting on the hard log, Tom peeked again from the woodshed. Everything was quiet. Tom left Thunder in the shed. "I'll be right back," he told him. "Don't bark."

He went to the kitchen door and looked through the glass pane. Tom could see evidence of the Bosworths' visit. Fiona was removing teacups from the table, along with a half loaf of molasses bread.

Enoch looked up from his seat at the table and motioned for Tom to come in. "They're gone," he said, as Tom entered the kitchen cautiously. "Amos and Bert wondered where you were."

"What did they want?" Tom asked.

"Amos is goin' huntin' next week way out beyond Blow-Me-Down Islands. He wondered if Ken Rideout and I want to go along with 'im."

"Are you goin'?" Tom asked.

"I could make some good money. There's a big

market for pelts and meat. We'll be on board a fine steel boat—can't be jammed on ice, you see." Enoch paused. "But I can't take you with me, Tom. I'll need you to stay here with Fiona."

"I'm not havin' this baby until April," she protested. "Tom might like to go with you."

"No," said Tom. "I'd rather stay with Fiona. How long will you be gone?"

"Between the hunt and business in St. John's before and after, we'll be gone a few weeks at the most," Enoch answered. "But I'm not sure I should go, with the baby comin' along so soon."

"Is Eddie goin' on the hunt?" Tom asked Enoch.

"No, he's stayin' at home to help out too. And so's Bert. Next year maybe they'll go."

"Don't worry about me, my love. I'll be fine with Tom," Fiona assured him. "And Margaret is just up the road."

"Well, then, I'll pack my things." Enoch got up from the table. "Amos and Bert are over to Ken's now. We're to meet at the waterfront within the hour and cross over to the mainland together."

"Enoch, do you think that Mr. Fowler will

show up to take Thunder while you're gone?" Tom asked.

"I doubt it, boy. It's only March, and we could have more snow yet. Besides, the ice is still in. He won't come until the mild weather."

Fiona helped Enoch to fill his nunny-bag with warm clothes, while Tom brought Thunder out from the woodshed.

"God be with you," Fiona said as she kissed Enoch good-bye. "And a good heavy hunt as well."

Enoch put his arm around Tom. "Take care of Fiona, won't you, my boy? We can't let anything happen to her or our baby."

"I'll take good care of them both," Tom promised.

Enoch patted Thunder's head and ruffled the fur around his neck. "And watch over them all, Thunder!" The dog's sleek, black body and tail wiggled eagerly.

Fiona and Tom stood waving with Thunder at the top of the hill. They watched the group of hunters silhouetted against the snowy harbor until they disappeared like shadows on the other side of the bay.

"They'll be goin' by boat once they get to Chance-Along. The water on the south harbor is open now," Fiona said. Tom could see concern in her eyes. "I hope they'll be safe."

"Enoch will be fine," Tom assured her. "He'll come home in no time at all."

"Let's storm the kettle," Fiona said. "I'll make tea and toast."

Once in the kitchen, Fiona went to the table. "Oh, m'lord. I forgot to put Enoch's compass in his nunny-bag."

"I'm sure the others brought compasses."

Fiona placed the compass on the kitchen shelf. Then she brought out a glass jar of partridgeberry jam and they sat at the table. "Remember when we picked these berries?"

"It was a right beautiful day. I can't wait for spring to come again."

"Neither can I, my dear," Fiona agreed. "I'm gettin' as fat as a pig. I'll be happy when the baby's born and the birds are singin' and the world is alive once more."

Thunder began to bark, then whine softly from the porch. Margaret Rideout came inside with her granny bag. "I'm here to see how that baby's doin'. It's been a while since we had a granny visit."

"I've never felt better," Fiona said. "But you're right; it is time for a checkup." She headed for the stairs, with Margaret at her heels. "I'll be back the once," she told Tom.

Tom went into the parlor and knelt by the cradle. He was proud of the work he and Enoch had put into the hard maple to make it smooth and beautiful. Tom picked up the soft, white sweater, bonnet, and booties that Fiona had made. How tiny they were! Soon there'd be a baby in this cradle. The whole idea was amazing.

He heard footsteps on the stairway. Tom got up as Margaret came into the parlor. She wasn't smiling. In fact she looked worried.

"Is everything all right?" Tom asked. Margaret didn't answer. "Is Fiona all right?" he asked again. "The baby?"

"They're both fine," Margaret said.

Fiona came into the room. Tom glanced from Fiona to Margaret. "If everyone is fine, why do you both look so scarified?"

"Nothin' for you to worry about, my child." Fiona gave a warning look to Margaret, who quickly lowered her eyes and fiddled with the handles on her granny bag.

"One day at a time," Margaret said too brightly. "That's the way to live. Things seem to take care of themselves when you take one day at a time."

Tom frowned. Why were they talking like that? "You'd best tell me what's worryin' you right now!"

Again Margaret and Fiona exchanged glances. "Tom's just a boy," Margaret said, shaking her head. "He shouldn't hear about having babies . . . and all that."

"Why not?" Tom exclaimed. "I'm old enough. I've seen cows birthin'. Besides, Enoch told me to take care of Fiona. How can I, if I don't know what's goin' on?"

Fiona nodded to Margaret. "Go ahead, tell him."

"All right, Tom," Margaret said. "Fiona and the baby are fine. It's just . . . well, the baby is breech."

"The baby is turned the wrong way to be born," Fiona explained. "It happens sometimes."

"What does it mean?" Tom asked.

"Maybe nothin' at all. Babies can be born breech. It's just a little more difficult, that's all," Fiona said.

"Fiona has another whole month to go," Margaret told him. "By then the little one should be headed in the proper direction."

"We'll be just fine, won't we, Margaret?" Fiona asked. "You've delivered breech babies before, haven't you?"

"Yes, I have." Margaret headed to the door. "But let's not plan on this little tyke comin' into the world backward! You've got a way to go, and things can change all around in a month." She pinched Tom's cheek. "You look right scared abroad!" she said. "Let's see a smile."

Tom pulled away. He sure didn't feel like smiling.

After Margaret left, Fiona said, "Don't borrow trouble, Tom. It's a while off before the baby comes." She looked tired. Fiona's belly was large, and she seemed out of breath lately. "I think I'll lie down on the couch for a while."

Tom plumped a pillow for her and then covered

her with an afghan. "Thank you, Tom. You're takin' good care of me." She yawned. "Carryin' this big baby around tuckers me out. I almost wish he—or she—would decide to come into the world right now."

"Not yet!" Tom exclaimed. "Not until April!"

During the next week Fiona seemed to be resting more than usual. In the mornings Tom would fill up the stove with brishney, get the fires crackling and the sparks darting up the chimney to the sky. Then he'd fill the kettle and set it simmering on the back of the stove.

Sometimes, if Fiona hadn't joined him in the kitchen by then, he'd take tea and toast on a tray up to the bedroom for her.

"You're spoilin' me!" she told him.

This morning was different, though. Fiona was downstairs before he was. "Look at the sunrise," she said. The eastern sky was ablaze—all scarlet and red, with patches of turquoise peeking through. "It's right gorgeous!"

"It's pretty," Tom agreed, "but red in the morning is the sign of a storm."

"Maybe it will rain," Fiona said.

Tom opened the porch door and a blast of icy air swept through the kitchen. "It's right cold outside," Tom said. "If it's a storm, it'll be snow, not rain. I'll fill the wood bin." Thunder was still curled up on his rug, his nose tucked between his paws. The dog lifted his head and watched Tom sleepily as he headed to the woodshed.

After breakfast the sun shone brightly, but rays of sunlight dipped down to the distant sea like streamers. "By jinkers! Take a look at those sun hounds! 'When the sun is drawing water, better bide home with your wife and daughter,'" Fiona quoted.

She put a chunk of salted pork into a pot and let it simmer on the stove. "Tonight will be Solomon Gosse's birthday!"

Tom grinned. There was nothing he loved to eat more than pork and cabbage, with lots of root vegetables, and a dessert of duff. Newfoundlanders called this banquet "Solomon Gosse's birthday."

Tom knew the Newfoundland tale of Solomon Gosse, the skipper of a fishing ship. Pork and vegetables along with a duff pudding was his crew's favorite meal and *always* served on Tuesday, Thursday, and Sunday. Once, when a cook served pork and duff on another day, he was asked why he had changed the tradition. "Because it's Solomon Gosse's birthday!" the cook replied, for lack of a better reason. From then on *any* pork and duff night became known as "Solomon Gosse's birthday."

Tom went to the shed and dug up a turnip, two beets, and some potatoes that had been kept cold and covered in dirt or paper since last summer. The chickens clucked and chattered at him as he threw seed into their feeder. Rufus made his usual complaints, crowing and charging at Tom. "Get out of here, Rufus," Tom yelled, kicking the bird away, "or you'll end up in a stew!" Tom took the vegetables into the kitchen and set them in the sink.

"I'm bringin' Thunder in to warm him up," Tom said, opening the door. Thunder trotted eagerly into the kitchen and plunked himself down by the fire. After Tom wiped up the wet paw prints, he set bowls of leftover biscuits with gravy and fresh water in front of the dog, who lapped the food noisily. His tail swished against Fiona's leg as she sat at the table.

Suddenly Fiona gasped.

"What's wrong?" Tom asked quickly. "Did Thunder hit you?"

She shook her head. "No, no. It's nothin'."

Tom took Thunder's food dish to the sink. "This dog sure was red-raw hungry, gobblin' up his food so fast!"

"I think I'll lie down for a while," Fiona said.

"I'll fire up the parlor stove."

"Thank you, my child." Fiona walked slowly into the next room, where she settled herself on the couch and closed her eyes. Tom tried to be quiet as he broke up kindling and stuffed it into the iron stove.

Fiona seemed to fall asleep, so Tom tiptoed back to the kitchen, poured himself more tea, and sat at the table. Thunder rested his big head on Tom's knee. "You're my best chum," he whispered to the dog. "My good boy."

Then Fiona called in an anxious voice. "Tom! I think we'd better get Margaret over here."

Tom jumped up. "I'll get her," he said. "Are you having the baby?"

"I—I don't know. But we better find out."

"Will you be all right while I'm gone?"

"I think so."

"I'll leave Thunder with you. If you get worse, send him to me. He knows his way to Margaret's." He pulled on his boots and grabbed his jacket. "I'll be back the once," Tom promised as he darted out the door.

He raced to the Rideouts' house, flew up the steps, and banged on the door. "Margaret! Margaret!" he yelled.

The door opened and Margaret looked out with surprise.

"It's Fiona!" Tom cried. "Come quick."

"You head back, Tom. I'll be right along!" Margaret grabbed her granny bag, then called to Eddie. "Watch Rowena, son. Fiona needs me!"

Tom ran home. He had hardly entered the house when Margaret came up behind him, her jacket open and her hair all windblown.

"In there," Tom said, and pointed to the parlor.

She went immediately to Fiona. Tom sat heavily in a chair. Sensing something to be wrong, Thunder sat by Tom and nudged his leg with a paw. When Tom stroked him, the dog leaned against him, whining softly.

"Oh, Thunder, Fiona *can't* be having the baby," Tom said. "She can't. It's too soon."

Tom couldn't make out what Margaret and Fiona were saying. Then, after several minutes, Tom went to the parlor door and called out, "Tell me what's goin' on!"

When Margaret finally came into the kitchen, she looked worried. "Tom, the baby wants to be born. He's not on his way yet, but he's still breech, and he's a big one. She's goin' to need a doctor. I wish I could get Doc Sullivan over here."

"I'll go get him," Tom offered.

"How? By the time you get across and back again, she may be . . . in real trouble."

Tom thought for a moment. "What if I put Fiona on the slide? Thunder and I can bring her to Dr. Sullivan's. He's just straight across the harbor."

"It's civil out there right now, Tom, but there may be a storm coming," Margaret said.

"If we hurry we could get over there before the storm."

"Do I have a few hours to go, Margaret?" Fiona asked, coming slowly into the kitchen.

"I think so. First babies are usually slower. It would save time to take you to the doctor, rather than bring him here."

"Tom, get the slide ready and harness up Thunder," Fiona said. "We're goin' across to Chance-Along!"

Margaret helped Fiona dress in Enoch's flannel shirt and breeches. She bundled her up, pulled a fur hat over her head, and wrapped a cloud—a soft, gauzy scarf—around her neck. Then Margaret stuffed a nunny-bag with molasses bread and a flask of hot tea. "I've put some 'lasses cookies in here for Thunder," Margaret said.

Tom dressed quickly. He found a pair of Enoch's boots with sparbles—metal brads on the soles that would keep him from slipping on the ice. The boots were too big, but fit better once Tom put on a pair of Enoch's heavy socks.

"Take the compass," Fiona said. "We might need it if it snows or we get fog."

Tom put the compass deep in his jacket

pocket. He hitched Thunder to the slide and fastened the booties Dr. Sullivan had made to protect the dog's paws. Thunder whined, trying to remove them with his teeth. "No!" Tom commanded. Thunder looked at Tom questioningly, but stopped pulling at the boots.

The sail on the sled would not be helpful if a storm came up, so after a moment's deliberation, he removed the canvas. "You've got *two* special passengers on board today, Thunder," Tom said. "We've got to get them safely to the doctor, so it's goin' to be all up to you!"

They walked down the hill to the frozen harbor. Tom could see that the mainland across the bay wasn't that far, really. They'd be fine.

Margaret helped Fiona into the slide, tucked a blanket around her, and tied the nunny-bag to the side of the sled. She hugged Fiona for a long moment. "Be strong, my girl. God bless you and your wee one."

Tom ran onto the harbor. "Come on, Thunder." He made a clicking sound with his tongue. "Let's go to Chance-Along!"

Thunder tugged hard at the sled. As it slid over the ice, he picked up speed and followed Tom, who trotted ahead.

They moved silently across the bay. In many places the gusty wind had blown the snow away, leaving slippery surfaces. Tom kept looking back to be sure that the slide didn't slip and tip over. Yet Thunder, with his harness taut and Dr. Sullivan's canvas mitts on his paws, kept moving ahead, smoothly and steadily.

After a while Tom paused to look up at the sky. Clouds had gathered, and he could feel spatters of snow against his face. Thunder stopped, waiting to see what Tom would do.

"I can't see the mainland," Fiona called. "It's snowing hard over there."

Tom peered to where he figured the shoreline should be, but it had disappeared!

"We'll keep going," he said, taking the compass from his pocket. The wavering arrow pointed behind him . . . to the north. This was correct. He needed to head south, and a little to the east. The wind blew in his face. "The storm's coming from the southeast," he told Fiona. "We're right on course." He clicked his tongue again. "Come on, Thunder."

The wind slapped the thickening snow onto their faces and clothing. This was no ordinary snowstorm. This was a blizzard!

Tom lowered his head as he headed into the gusts. Fiona had pulled her scarf around her face. *Just keep moving*, Tom thought. *Into the wind.*

The snow swirled around them in a ghostly dance. It was hard to see anything. Tom searched for the shoreline. Surely it couldn't be too far away now. If he could just see the flicker of a light—any light—just to show a sign of human life. But there was nothing in any direction except snow and a shrieking wind.

"Tom! I can't see anything but snow." Fiona's scarf muffled her voice.

"Are *you* all right?" Tom asked.

When she didn't answer, Tom moved closer to the slide. Fiona had her hand over her mouth and her eyes were closed. "Are you all right?" he repeated.

She nodded. "Keep going, Tom."

He paused to brush the thick snow from Fiona's blanket and then from Thunder's fur. "Come on, boy." Thunder, head down, plodded on, but he was panting, and his pace was slow as he pushed against the wind.

They started off again. The blinding snow froze on Tom's eyelashes. It seemed over an hour since they had left Back o' the Moon, yet the opposite shore was still out of sight. At times Tom could hardly see the sled. It was as if the world had disappeared and they were trapped in a snowy dream, racing to nowhere.

How much farther? Tom wondered. He, too, was tiring. Then he had a frightening thought. He'd been using the wind for direction, but what if the wind had shifted? They could be going in circles. He reached for the compass to take another look. It wasn't in his pocket. He tried the other pocket, then all the pockets on his jacket and pants. The compass was gone! It must have dropped out somewhere! He stopped, his heart racing, his breath panting.

"Why have you stopped?" Fiona called. "We've got to get across soon!"

Tom just couldn't tell Fiona the compass was gone. She'd think he was a stupid gommel! Thunder had stopped and was licking at a front paw. Tom lifted the paw—the mitt had fallen off somewhere, and now there was blood on the pads of the dog's foot.

Tom reached for the nunny-bag tied to the side of the sled. "I need somethin' for Thunder's paw. It's bleedin'," he told Fiona.

"Here, tear off a snig from my cloud." She handed her scarf to him. "It's soft."

Tom ripped off one end of the scarf and tied it to Thunder's paw. He gave the scarf back to Fiona, then pulled some cookies out of the nunny-bag for Thunder, who devoured them instantly. "Good boy," he said. "Good dog." Turning to Fiona he asked, "Would tea warm you up?"

"Tea? No, Tom. We can't stop now."

"Come on, boy. Come on, Thunder." Tom clicked his tongue and headed into the wind.

They trudged on, slower than before. Suddenly Thunder swerved, and Fiona shrieked as the sled tilted, then righted itself.

The red-and-white harbor markers, pointing

the way around the shoals, were frozen in the ice directly in front of them!

"Fiona! It's the markers!" Tom yelled. "We're almost there!"

"Oh, thanks be to God!"

Tom began to run. "Come on, Thunder!"

Thunder followed after him, then stopped and began to bark. "Oh, what's wrong?" Tom asked impatiently. "Come on, boy. Just a little way and we'll be there." He tried to urge Thunder on, but the dog refused to budge.

In a sudden gust of wind, the snow cleared. Just ahead of them Tom could see a stream of open water!

"Tom!" Fiona shrieked. "There's only water ahead!"

"There's a strong current here. It's taken the ice out," Tom said, remembering Enoch's warning when they had crossed earlier in the winter. *In the spring, the currents shift beneath the ice and could leave you stranded, or you could fall through and drown.*

"What'll we do?" Fiona cried. "We could be carried out to sea if we're on an ice pan."

"We're not. We're on the stable side," Tom insisted. "You saw the markers. They're right where they're supposed to be, and anchored to the bottom." If only the storm would stop, maybe someone would see the slide and rescue them.

"Perhaps we could follow the water," suggested

Fiona. "It may end somewhere, and then we could cross."

Tom nodded. "Which way, though? The stream heads from west to east, heading out to sea."

"Head west. That's safer. Let me see the compass."

Tom didn't answer. Instead he said, "We'll turn to our right—that's west—and follow the stream of water for a while."

"Check the compass, Tom," Fiona said.

"I can't," Tom finally admitted. "I lost it somewhere."

Fiona was silent. Tom wouldn't have blamed her if she had yelled and screamed at him. He promised Enoch he'd take care of her and the baby, and here they were, stranded on the ice!

"Well, Tom, no sense in troublin' ourselves about the compass," Fiona finally said. "If it's gone, it's gone. We'll just have to get along without it. Thunder has good instincts. He'll find a way to cross. We've got to trust him and move on."

They followed the stream of open water in what seemed to be a westerly direction. There *had* to be a place to cross.

They were only walking now. Thunder was too tired to run. "If we keep heading this way, we might come to the causeway between the mainland and the island," Fiona said. "Even though the bridge is out, we'd be closer to shore."

"That's right," Tom agreed. But he wondered if the ice was gone there, too.

Fiona suddenly let out a cry of pain. Tom stopped. "It's all right, Tom," she said quickly. "Just keep goin'."

Tom was praying with every breath. *Help us find our way to the doctor! Help us! Help us!*

It was hard to tell just how long they'd been on the westerly course when Tom saw the open water narrowing, then closing. Could they cross now? Was it an ice pan over there that might take them out to sea? They stopped. The ice was black—unsafe. Thunder stopped and sniffed at the ice, then backed away, whining.

"We can't cross here," Tom said. "It may be stronger farther down."

They finally found a section of white ice that seemed safe. Tom walked out on it and jumped several times. It sounded hollow like a drum, and he wasn't sure. He examined the ice carefully. It looked strong. But still . . .

"What'll we do?" But when he looked up, Thunder had already gone ahead with the slide and was heading off to the south again. Or was it the south?

Thunder knows it's safe, Tom thought. *And he knows where we're goin'.* Tom ran to catch up. "Thunder! Wait for me!"

Then, through the blustering snow, Tom finally saw a faint light in the distance. The shore of the mainland!

"There's land ahead!" Fiona had seen it too.

The light became brighter, and now they could see houses. Flankers sparked out of chimneys, then faded.

"We must not have gone too far west, because there's Dr. Sullivan's," Tom called. Thunder barked and began to trot again. "Thunder knew just where to go!"

Once they reached the mainland, Tom helped Thunder pull the slide onto the shore. "I'll get help," Tom told Fiona. He raced to Dr. Sullivan's and banged on the door.

The doctor came out to help Fiona into the house. Breathlessly Tom explained why they were there.

"Unbelievable!" the doctor exclaimed, after hearing Tom's hurried story. "Take a rest, Tom. And try not to worry about Fiona. I'll do the best I can to help her and the baby." He went quickly into another room where Fiona was already waiting.

Dr. Sullivan's housekeeper, Mrs. Jenkins, heated up chicken soup. "Tom, my boy, you and your dog are true heroes, comin' across the bay in a blizzard!" She set two big bowls of soup in front of Tom and Thunder. "Eat up! And don't be scarified about your ma. She's in good hands and everything's goin' to be all right."

"Fiona's not my ma," Tom said. "My name's Tom Campbell. I just live with the Murrays."

"She's not your ma?" Mrs. Jenkins said in surprise. "I thought sure you were her son. You seem so close—as if you're family." She sliced bread and put it on the table.

"I wish Fiona really was my ma," Tom said. Then, feeling his face flush, he began to eat. Thunder had already gulched down his food and was tearing the booties off his paws. Mrs. Jenkins noticed the bloody scarf on his foot and brought out some ointment. "You put this on the dog's paws, my boy," she said, handing the can to Tom. "He'll be fine in the mornin'."

Gently Tom patted the salve on Thunder's paw pads. Thunder tried to lap it off. "No, Thunder," Tom scolded.

Thunder crawled under the table, curled up, and was soon snoring.

Tom sank into an immense lounge chair in

Dr. Sullivan's parlor, his head on a pillow, a quilt over him, and his feet propped up on a leather footstool.

He could hear quiet voices, doors opening and shutting, a cry now and then that he recognized as coming from Fiona. *Lord, please let them be all right.* Slowly Tom slipped into a restless sleep.

Tom awakened when Dr. Sullivan touched his arm. "Come with me," he said to Tom. Dr. Sullivan's sleeves were rolled up and there were spatters of blood on his white jacket and trousers. His forehead was sweaty and he looked exhausted.

Tom threw aside the quilt and followed the doctor down the hallway. "Is Fiona all right?"

"See for yourself." Dr. Sullivan gestured to a small room beyond the kitchen. Thunder crept out from under the table and followed Tom. "I don't usually let dogs into the patient's room," Dr. Sullivan said, "but Thunder isn't just any dog."

Fiona was in a bed by the window. She turned her head and smiled weakly at Tom and Thunder. "Just look what I have here."

Tom tiptoed across the room. Tucked next to her was a small bundle. Tom peered closer and Fiona pulled the blanket away to reveal a rosy little face. Long lashes fringed the baby's closed eyes and the tiny lips reminded Tom of pink satin ribbon.

"Would you like to kiss your sister, Tom?" Fiona asked. "I'm right sure she wants to thank her big brother for bein' so brave and gettin' us here safely."

Tom bent over and kissed the soft golden fuzz on the baby's head. He touched her hand and the baby grasped his finger. Tom exclaimed. "She knows me!"

"'Course she does." Fiona smiled at Thunder. "Lo and behold you, Thunder! What a clever, good dog you are." Thunder's tail wagged.

"What's the baby's name?" Tom asked.

"April—even though she was born in March." Fiona was pale, and dark circles shadowed her eyes.

"Are you sure you're all right?" Tom asked.

"Dr. Sullivan says I'll be fine in a week or two. This baby was some real hard work, let me tell."

Tom looked out the window. It was dark and the snow had finally stopped. A full moon cast the shadows of trees on the new-fallen snow. "What time is it?"

Fiona pointed to a clock on the wall. "Four o'clock in the morning." She tucked the blanket around the baby and kissed her cheek. "Tom, please put April over there." She gestured to a crib in the corner.

"I've never held a baby before," Tom told Fiona as she placed April in his arms. He took small, cautious steps as he carried the tiny bundle, then gently set her down in the crib. She was asleep and stirred a bit. "She's so beautiful," said Tom.

"She sure is. Truer words were never spoke. It's been a long day and night. I hope you can get some rest, son." Fiona closed her eyes and was soon asleep.

Tom tiptoed out of the room with Thunder at his heels. He found Dr. Sullivan at the kitchen table with a mug in his hand. "Have some tea, my boy," he said.

Tom poured a cup for himself and sat down.

Thunder came over and nuzzled his head under Tom's arm. "You're sure Fiona and the baby are doin' well?"

"Fit as a fiddle, both of them. But it was a hard birth, you see. Between us and all harm, that's a big baby in there!"

April didn't seem big. In fact she looked right tiny to Tom.

"Margaret Rideout did the proper thing, sendin' you all over here," Dr. Sullivan said.

"How long will Fiona have to stay here?"

"She needs time to get stronger, lad." Dr. Sullivan went to the kitchen dresser and brought out a dish of ginger snaps that he offered to Tom. "I hear tell that Enoch is on a hunt. He'll be stunned as an owl when he meets his new little girl!"

Tom helped himself to a cookie. "He won't be back for another week or two. I don't know where I can stay in the meanwhiles. Or where Fiona and the baby can stay once she's better. We can't go back to the island while the ice is breakin' up."

"Do you know someone here in Chance-Along who'd take you in?"

"No, sir. And don't forget I have Thunder with me. I need to keep him out of sight in Chance-Along 'cause someone might steal him for Mr. Fowler's reward."

"Aye. Don't worry 'bout a blessed thing," said the doctor. "I know someone who'll be glad to help."

Dawn was just creeping into the sky when Tom fell asleep again on the big chair in the parlor.

It was almost noon when Tom woke up. Some patients were sitting nearby, waiting to see the doctor. Tom was so embarrassed he wanted to hide under the quilt. Had he snored? His tongue was dry, and he wondered if his mouth had been open while these folks were watching him.

"Excuse me," he muttered. One man chuckled as Tom got up and went to the kitchen. Thunder was whining by the door, so Tom let him out into the yard.

Dr. Sullivan had bandaged his sore paw, and Thunder limped a bit as he walked around, sniffing every unfamiliar tree. Tom stayed with him for a few minutes, then brought him inside again.

Mrs. Jenkins shook her head at the wet paw prints on her kitchen floor.

"I'll clean them up," Tom offered.

She handed him a rag. "I guess that dog has a right to leave tracks after bringin' Mrs. Murray over from the island through the storm."

After Tom wiped the floor, Mrs. Jenkins made him fish 'n' brewis with scrunchions—salt pork fried until it was crunchy and crisp. Tom glutched it down as if he'd never eaten a thing in his life.

Later he and Thunder peeked into Fiona's room. The baby was crying, her tiny fists pounding the air, her small face red and crinkled. "Is she all right?" Tom asked.

"Bring her to me, Tom," Fiona said.

Holding his breath, Tom lifted the wiggling baby and carried her across the room to Fiona. Fiona hoisted April over her shoulder and patted the baby's back until she burped.

"That was a loud burp for such a wee one," Tom said with a laugh.

Thunder rested his chin on Fiona's bed. Fiona held the baby up to Thunder. "Here's our baby that you saved, you clever fellow." Thunder sniffed curiously at April, then wagged his tail.

Fiona cradled April in her arms and sang soft cheek music. "I dee diddily diddily dum, I dee diddily dide." The baby gurgled, then gradually closed her eyes. "Good wee babe," Fiona whispered. She turned to Tom and spoke softly. "Tom, Dr. Sullivan talked with me. There's a place for us to stay while we're here waitin' for Enoch to come back, or for the ice to go out—whichever comes first."

"When shall I go?"

"Today. April and I will come next week when I'm better." Fiona looked anxious. "The doctor will tell you all about it. These people want us, Tom. They want to help us, including Thunder. It will be all right. Please trust me and Doc Sullivan," she pleaded.

Why was Fiona saying all this? Then Tom suddenly realized—they were moving in with the Bosworths!

at three o'clock in the afternoon, Bert and Ruby showed up at Dr. Sullivan's. Ruby carried a small package done up with pink ribbons.

"You're comin' home with us," Bert said as soon as he saw Tom.

"Well, that's some invite!" Ruby exclaimed, poking Bert with her elbow. "You've got some things to say to Tom, so speak up! Meanwhile, I'm goin' to see Fiona and that baby." She headed down the hall.

Bert took off his cap and shuffled his feet. "Guess we made a fine kettle of fish for you and the dog."

"I'll go bail for that!" Tom replied.

"Me and Pa were as foolish as caplin."

Tom smiled a little. Caplin were stupid fish that

just ran straight to shore and could often be caught by hand. "Yep. Foolish as caplin," he agreed.

"Well, anyway, you might as well stay with us. We can hide Thunder while you're in town."

Tom shrugged. "I guess I'll have to—at least until we can go back to the island." He gave Bert a long look. "I've heard that a man from the States is coming here to get Thunder."

"Maybe he won't show up," Bert said. He waited, then sighed when Tom didn't respond. "How about us gettin' you a little crackie? Everyone loves crackies. They're only mongrels, but they're clever and cute, and small enough to hold in your lap! My uncle's dog is goin' to have puppies. He said he'd give you one."

"I don't want a crackie. I only want Thunder."

Ruby peeked out from Fiona's room and waved her hand to the boys. "Come see the baby."

As they walked down the hall Bert said, "So what's the baby's name?"

"April."

"April? Why did they name her that?"

"She was to be born in April."

"Well, then, she should really be named March!"

Bert guffawed, trying to be funny. "March Murray."

You really are as foolish as a caplin, Tom wanted to say. But he bit his tongue.

Fiona was holding a lacy white dress and bonnet. "Tom, look what Ruby brought for April. Isn't it lovely?"

"It was Nancy's when she was a baby," Ruby said. "She only wore it once, for her christening."

"It's even more beautiful, knowing it was once Nancy's. Thank you." Fiona looked up at Bert. "Come see our baby, Bert."

Bert peered into the blanket at April. "She's real little, ain't she?"

"She's the image of Fiona," Ruby said. "Just look at that golden hair."

"Fiona," Bert said abruptly, "Tom and Thunder are comin' to home with us."

Fiona gave Tom a relieved smile. "Thank you." Tom wasn't sure if she was thanking Bert or him.

The Bosworths were now living in a large apartment above Bert's uncle's hardware store. It had three bedrooms and a bathroom. It seemed that they had received some money from the government and from relief funds to help with their losses. Tom wondered if Enoch and Fiona could get some help too.

"I went to the Salvationists and found clothes that should fit you and Fiona," Ruby said. "People from all over Newfoundland sent them to the outports that were destroyed."

"It'll feel good to take a bath and change into clean clothes," Tom said.

Bert took Tom and Thunder to the back porch and then down a flight of steps to the closed-in yard. "Thunder'll be safe here," Bert said. "We'll bring 'im up to the porch at night." Bert patted Thunder's back. "We're tryin' to rightify things, Thunder. We don't want you to be taken away from Tom."

Tom was to sleep on a cot in Bert's room. Bert was proud to show off the electric lights. "See? Just pop the switch and there's light. Betcha never saw anythin' like this before."

"Chance-Along sure is modern compared to Back o' the Moon," Tom said. Bert sounded so proud, Tom didn't want to spoil things by telling Bert that they had electricity back at the mission. "Where's Nancy?" he asked.

"In school," Bert answered. "I might be goin' to school someday." He took a paper and pencil from a shelf. "Watch me write both my names." Tom looked on as Bert slowly wrote in large letters: BERT BOSWORTH.

"That's right good, Bert."

"Wanna see how I write *fish* now?" Again, Bert's fingers moved awkwardly with the pencil, but the letters were clear: FISH.

"Watch *this*!" This time Bert wrote: CODFISH.

"Pretty clever, eh? I figured that one out myself," Bert said proudly.

"Where did you learn that?" Tom asked.

"Nancy helped a little. She's doin' good in school. Nancy's teacher said she was taught by a real good honker."

"Honker?"

"You know—uh—tooter. That's you, Tom."

"Oh, a tutor!" Tom said with a laugh. "I've never been called a honker or tooter in all my born days!"

a week later Fiona was well enough to leave Dr. Sullivan's and move in with the Bosworths. Everyone was excited when they heard the news.

"I want to share my room with April," Nancy whined. "Bert has Tom. I want April."

"She's too little, Nance," Ruby said. "She needs to be with her ma. You and I will share my room and Fiona and April will have your room."

Nancy pouted for the rest of the morning.

"What'll we do when Pa comes home, and Enoch?" Bert asked.

"We'll figure it all out then," Ruby answered. "I hear tell the ice is out in Rumble Reach."

"When I was at Doc's earlier I could see clear across. There were white horses on the bay." Tom had been excited to see the deep water tipped with whitecaps instead of gray ice. "The only way home now is by boat," said Tom. "I hope we can go back soon." It had been hard to keep a dog the size of a small pony in a fenced-in yard, and Thunder was used to more freedom.

At noontime Dr. Sullivan arrived in his carriage with Fiona and April. "It was a bumpy ride, I'm afraid," said Dr. Sullivan. "We're in mud season now."

"April seemed to like it," said Fiona. "She's fast asleep."

Ruby took the baby, and Dr. Sullivan helped Fiona from the carriage.

"Thank you for all you've done, Doctor." Fiona kissed the doctor's cheek and shook his hand.

"Good luck to all of you," Dr. Sullivan said as he rode away.

Ruby helped Fiona get her things settled in Nancy's room. She had lined a wooden biscuit box with a soft blanket, as a bed for April. "Empty biscuit boxes are used for most everything," she said to Fiona. "Whenever Amos sees a new house he says 'It's prob'ly made from biscuit boxes.'"

Ruby brought the box into the kitchen. "Now come along and have a bite." Ruby placed the baby in the biscuit box next to Fiona, then set a huge platter of pork sandwiches and bowls of applesauce on the table.

Nancy sat on the floor, admiring the baby. "She's like a dolly. She's the prettiest baby I've ever seen in all my born days."

They were just about to eat when Thunder barked excitedly from the porch. Suddenly the door burst open. Enoch and Amos stepped into the kitchen.

"We're back!" Amos yelled. "And thanks be to God, we had a good hunt!"

Enoch ran to Fiona. "Oh, thank the good Lord you're safe," he said, kissing her. "I heard about your ordeal when we tied up in port."

Fiona took April from the box. "Here's your little daughter, April," she said tenderly.

Enoch held the baby gently. "She's a beauty," Enoch whispered. "Like her mother." Tom could see Enoch's eyes fill with tears. "I can't believe all that's happened and I wasn't here. . . ." He kissed April's golden hair.

"Where's Ken?" Bert asked. "Ain't he with you?"

"He got a ride home to Back o' the Moon. The harbor's open now," Amos replied.

Enoch turned to Tom. "From what I hear tell, you saved Fiona and the baby." He held April with one arm and hugged Tom with the other. "Just sayin' thank you isn't enough, Tom. You're a true blessin' to us, son."

"I promised I'd take care of Fiona."

"And that you did, my boy." Enoch kissed the baby's cheek. "I shouldn't even touch her," he said, handing her back to Fiona. "I just got off the ship—dirty duds—a right slattery slob. But couldn't wait to see you . . . both of you."

Both of you, Enoch had said. That meant Fiona and April, not Tom. *When would he stop feeling left out?* Tom wondered.

"You men wash up and then come eat with us," Ruby ordered. "Don't make shy, Enoch. This is your home as long as you're here."

While they were eating, Fiona and Tom told

everyone about their journey from the island. As they described the blinding snow, the open water, and Fiona so close to having the baby, Enoch and Amos shook their heads in disbelief.

"Between us and all harm!" Amos said. "That's a wilder story than we've got to tell."

"Tom and Thunder made it turn out well," said Enoch, "with a darlin' little bonus, to boot." He smiled at the baby in the box and took hold of Fiona's hand. "I'm sorry I wasn't here to help you."

"I wished you were here too," Fiona said, "but Tom and Thunder never gave up."

"They took care o' things right well," Amos agreed. "And no one tried to steal Thunder?"

"Not a one," Ruby said. "I'm sure most folks here in Chance-Along know what a hero that dog is."

"There's no one with a heart so hard that they'd take Thunder away from us," Fiona said.

Amos sighed. "I was right ascared that he'd be stolen. That's why at Christmastime I went with me brother and his friends to warn ya."

Enoch and Fiona gasped, and Tom's mouth dropped open.

"*You* were the mummers?" Fiona asked.

"I was the Fool. And a fool I truly was—causin' all that trouble about Thunder." Amos looked down at his feet. "I . . . didn't have the nerve to come out and admit it, so I decided to warn ya from behind the Fool's mask."

"So it was you all the time," Enoch said. "Well, we did keep a close watch on Thunder 'cause of your warnin'."

"But that Mr. Fowler will be comin' anyway," Tom said. "And we can't hide from *him*."

"We'll try to help you keep Thunder in any way we can," Ruby said.

Enoch and Amos then told about their successful hunt. "The establishment bought everything, all the meat and pelts. We've got enough money to get us by for a good spell," Enoch said, "and perhaps some left over so we can all pitch in on a fishin' boat later."

"And on the way back we happenstanced upon a nice bull moose for ourselves," Amos said. "We'll have meat to last until May."

After eating, Enoch and Amos told about their plans. "We've decided to keep on workin' with each other, includin' Ken Rideout," Amos announced.

"A partnership?" Fiona asked. "That should help us all get by."

"We've all been offered jobs at the fishery here in Chance-Along," Enoch said. "So if a partnership can't be worked out, we'll be able to get work here."

"I'd hate to leave Back o' the Moon," Fiona said.

"And I'd hate to give up my independence," Enoch stated.

"Things will work out, won't they?" Fiona asked.

"We'll be fine," Enoch said. "While we're here in Chance-Along I'm goin' to send a telegram to the Earthquake Relief Fund and see about gettin' us a boat—even a small one—just to get around in for now. They'll help us with the costs." Enoch looked at Fiona and winked. "And we have other business to attend to, don't we, maid?"

"Yes, indeed," Fiona answered with a smile meant only for Enoch.

Tom looked down at his hands, trying not to notice. *They have a secret*, he thought. *And it doesn't include me.*

the next morning Enoch took Tom and Thunder with him while he bought a boat along with a small engine. Tom felt more secure bringing Thunder to town. Hadn't Ruby assured him that everyone in Chance-Along who had heard about Thunder's trek through the blizzard with Fiona would protect the dog? Still, Tom kept Thunder close by his side.

While they were negotiating the price of the boat with the owner, Thunder barked and leaped aboard. "See? Your dog knows this is a nice tight little vessel for the money," the man said with a laugh.

"We'll take it," Enoch said. He seemed pleased. "This boat's big enough to carry us all to Back o' the Moon," he said to Tom. "We can fish with it too."

When they returned to the Bosworths' apartment and told Amos about the new boat, he said, "I thought we were goin' to take on with each other."

"Maybe we will. In the meantime I'll need a boat," Enoch said. "We'll work out the partnership with that lawyer, Mr. Robinson, once we get settled. Then, if we have enough money between us, we'll pitch in together three ways for a bigger boat."

"We don't need a lawyer," Amos grumbled.

"Yes, we do," Enoch insisted. "It's the only way to do business proper."

It's the only way to do business with Amos, Tom thought.

"This afternoon Fiona and I have an appointment with Mr. Robinson," Enoch said. "I'd like you to come with us, Tom."

"Why are you goin' to a lawyer?" Tom asked. "And why do you want me to go with you?"

"We've got some business to attend to, and we'd like you to be there," Enoch told him.

"We'll get a bite to eat at the Copper Kettle, too. You'd like that, wouldn't you, Tom?" Fiona asked.

Tom nodded eagerly. "Sounds like fun," he agreed.

That afternoon Fiona wore one of Ruby's Sunday-go-to-meeting dresses, and Enoch put on some new pants and a jacket that Ruby had found for Amos at the Salvationists' store. "Perfect fit," Enoch said.

"You're about the same size as Amos," Ruby explained.

"Here, Tom, wear these." Fiona held up a pair of navy pants, a plaid shirt, and a pair of shiny shoes, also from the Salvationists. "They look span-new!"

"We're not goin' to church. Why are we dressin' up?" Tom asked.

"We want to look respectable at the lawyer's," she answered.

"What about the baby? And Thunder?"

"Ruby will mind April and Thunder."

As soon as Tom was ready, they went down-street to the center of town, where Mr. Robinson had his office. Tom could see his reflection in the store windows as they passed. He hardly recognized himself all dressed up. Fiona looked beautiful in Ruby's green dress, with her hair falling over her shoulders like sunshine. And Enoch seemed especially tall and handsome today. But why they were going to a lawyer was still a mystery to Tom.

They sat in the waiting room until Mr. Robinson called them into his office. The afternoon sun reflected on the dark, polished wood of the large desk by the window.

Another man was standing in the office whom Mr. Robinson introduced as Judge Shipton. "Judge Shipton makes trips to Chance-Along once a year," he explained. "He represents His Majesty's judicial system in Newfoundland and travels from St. John's to different parts of the island to take care of all sorts of legal issues."

Legal issues?

The judge was a small man with a kind face and eyes that crinkled when he smiled. "Welcome," he said, shaking hands with Fiona and Enoch. "And this must be Thomas Campbell. I've heard a lot about you, laddie." He put his arm around Tom's shoulder and led him to a leather chair next to the big desk. He motioned Fiona and Enoch to the other two chairs.

Judge Shipton sat down at Mr. Robinson's desk and folded his hands. The lawyer stood nearby. "This is a special day for you, Tom," the judge began. "Mr. and Mrs. Murray have made a request to the courts of Newfoundland regarding you."

"Me?" Tom's voice squeaked.

"They would like to adopt you as their own son."

For a moment Tom couldn't speak. Then he stammered, "*Adopt me*? . . . You mean . . . Fiona would be my . . . real . . . ma . . . and . . . Enoch would be my pa?"

The lawyer nodded. "But only if you want this, Tom."

Enoch spoke up. "When we were in Chance-Along last fall we talked with Mr. Robinson about adoptin' you. But we weren't sure we'd be allowed to. We wondered if perhaps we weren't . . . well, good enough."

"Good enough! No one could be as good as you've been to me," said Tom.

At his words, Fiona's eyes brightened with tears. "We wanted to tell you real bad, so you'd know and believe how much we love you, Tom. But we didn't want you to be disappointed if things went wrong."

"You see, we had to have consent of the court," Enoch said. "They wanted to know lots of things about *us* first."

"Enoch and Fiona wrote a letter saying how much they wanted you as their son. That—along with a lot of paperwork—convinced the courts in St. John's that they'd make good parents," Mr. Robinson explained.

"Mr. and Mrs. Murray have been approved," the judge announced. "But there's one more important thing, Tom. Do *you* want this? Do you want to be their real son?"

"Tom, you won't be Thomas Campbell any longer. You'll be Thomas Murray," Mr. Robinson told him.

"Thomas Campbell Murray," Fiona said. "You won't be giving up your own parents or heritage. That'll never change."

"It's all up to you, Tom," said Enoch. "You may need to think about this for a while. So go ahead; take your time."

Tom thought about his parents. They seemed like a distant dream now. He was still connected to them, but their faces had become shadows, along with the fading but loving memories.

"I don't need any time," Tom said, glancing at Fiona and Enoch, who were holding hands. His eyes filled with tears. "I want to be Thomas Campbell Murray."

"Done!" Judge Shipton decreed, tapping a gavel on the desk. "From now on that's who you are: Thomas Campbell Murray."

Tom stood up as Fiona and Enoch came across the room and threw their arms around him. "We love you, son" Fiona said, kissing his forehead.

"I love *you*," said Tom.

the Murray family headed home to Back o' the
Moon in April.

The Rideouts ran down to greet them at the
new dock near their house. "Welcome to home!"
they called. "You're a sight for sore eyes!"

"Oh, God's blessin' on this sweet child,"
Margaret said, taking the baby from Fiona. "To
think we might have lost her!" She studied April's
face. "How right beautiful she is."

Thunder bounded out of the boat and headed
up the hill to the house, sniffing everywhere, as if
to be sure he was really home.

The island was coming to life with budding
leaves and grass. The house was as they left it, the
soot and ashes still in the stoves from the last
fires. Fiona's pot of salt pork was empty, cleaned

and set on the kitchen dresser. "We ate the pork," Margaret told them. "Couldn't let it go to waste!"

"But we kept Rufus," Eddie added with a laugh. "He's a tough old bird, so we decided not to eat him."

Tom's pocket watch was on his bureau. He wound it, then placed it in his pocket. "It's good to be home," Tom said again and again. This really *was* his home. Thomas Campbell Murray's home!

It took a couple of weeks for everything to get back to normal. Amos borrowed his brother's boat to bring lumber over for the Murrays' new wharf, and Enoch, Ken, and Amos started putting the dock together for the Murrays' boat. Tom, Eddie, and Bert were assigned to waterproof the underpinnings with a black tarry paint.

"Watch me read the label on the can," Eddie said. "Gib-son's Dock Paint. Guaran-teed water proof." He looked pleased with himself. "See?" he said to Bert. "Tom taught me to read this winter. Ma and Pa were right surprised at Christmas when I read to them."

"I can read and write . . . a little," Bert said.

"Maybe you'll teach me to read better. Will ya, Tom?"

"Sure," Tom said. "We got the whole summer ahead of us." He looked up from his work to see Amos and Enoch off by themselves, talking seriously. Enoch glanced over at Tom several times. Finally Enoch motioned for Tom to come over.

"What's wrong?" Tom asked, walking over to them, the paintbrush still in his hand.

"You tell 'im," Amos said. "I ain't good at this."

With a sudden chill, Tom knew what he was about to hear. "Mr. Fowler's comin' for Thunder," Tom said. "Isn't he?"

Enoch nodded.

"When?"

"This afternoon."

"He can't!" Tom screamed, throwing the paintbrush onto the rocks.

"What's wrong with you?" Eddie asked him.

"Leave 'im alone," said Bert. "It's bad news. That Mr. Fowler's comin' to get Thunder."

"What are you goin' to do?" Eddie looked horrified. "You can't let 'im take Thunder!"

"I know what we'll do," Tom answered. "We'll

run away. We'll hide and no one will ever find us!
Come on, Thunder!" The dog jumped up and followed as Tom flew up the path to the house.

Fiona was in the rocking chair on the porch,
nursing April. "What's wrong?"

"Mr. Fowler's comin' to take Thunder away!"

Fiona's face paled. "Oh, no! Oh, Tom!"

"We're gonna run away. We're gonna hide. He
can't take Thunder from me."

"Tom, don't be so upset," Fiona begged. "Try to
think how happy Mr. Fowler will be to see his dog
again. And how sad he must have been to lose him."

Enoch, who had raced after Tom, entered the
yard. "Tom, let's go inside and talk about this."

"Can we buy 'im? You said maybe we'd offer
money for Thunder."

"Tom, you know that most of our money has
gone into the boat and the wharf. There's no way
we can pay for a prize dog like Thunder. Besides, if
Mr. Fowler's comin' all the way from Massachusetts
down in the States, then he must want his dog real
fierce."

Tom sat on the porch steps, put his arms
around Thunder, and cried into the white streak

on the dog's chest. "You're my clever, good dog. You don't want to leave me, do you?" He smothered his face in Thunder's furry neck and sobbed. "I won't let them take you. I won't!" He looked up at Amos, who had come up to the house. "Did you tell Mr. Fowler how to get here?"

"Not me, boy. But someone on the mainland gave him directions."

"It's all your fault," Tom yelled at Amos. "You're a spiteful, jealous, mean man!" Tom ran into the house, holding the door open for Thunder. "Come on, boy!" He raced up the stairs to his room. Thunder, having never been allowed up the stairs before, stopped, then sat on the hooked rug at the foot of the stairway.

Tom lay on the bed looking up at the ceiling. He had prayed so often to keep Thunder, and now he was going to lose him anyway.

Enoch came into the room and sat at the foot of the bed. "I know how you're feelin'." Tom didn't speak, so Enoch went on. "Tom, you can recite all the Ten Commandments by heart. You must remember the one that says it isn't right to covet what belongs to someone else."

"Amos and Bert coveted Thunder."

"That's right, and look at the trouble it's caused, lad." Enoch was quiet for a moment. Then he said, "Tom, you might ask yourself if you're unhappy because you know Thunder rightfully belongs to Mr. Fowler."

Tom turned away. "I don't want to talk about it."

"Perhaps God sent Thunder to you in that storm because you needed him. And look what he's done. He saved Rowena, Fiona, April. He saved us from the church spire collapsing on us during the earthquake, and he warned everyone about the tidal wave. Most of all, he brought us together, as a family."

"If God sent him, why is He taking him away?"

"Because it's time. And now we need to do what's right." Enoch got up to leave the room. "I know you'll do the right thing, Tom." He closed the door quietly.

tom was sitting on the porch with Thunder and Fiona when a sleek white yacht came into Rumble Reach and pulled up to the Rideouts' wharf.

"Take a look at that beauty," Fiona said. "Never saw the likes!"

Amos and Bert came running up from where they had been working on the new dock. "It's him!" Bert yelled. "I know it's him. No one from around these parts has a ship like that!"

Thunder sat up and barked at the excitement.

"Enoch's goin' over to meet 'im," Amos said. "He'll bring 'im over here."

"Do somethin'!" Bert ordered. "Hide the dog!"

Tom got up and went into the parlor. He didn't want to be around the Bosworths. Especially now.

He peeked out the window and saw Bert and Amos patting Thunder and talking to each other. Fiona followed Tom inside, and the two of them sat together on the couch. She held his hand as they waited quietly for Enoch and Mr. Fowler.

The parlor clock ticked loudly as they waited, each minute seeming like an age. Yet Thunder was silent now. Did he recognize Mr. Fowler and that's why he wasn't barking?

Enoch came in the house with a tall, slim gentleman. "This is Mr. Fowler," he said, introducing the man to Fiona and Tom.

As Mr. Fowler shook Tom's hand, he said, "Your father told me how well you've taken care of my dog."

"Thunder took good care of *us*," Tom answered.

"I've heard stories from everyone about Shadow," he said. "That's what I call him. When he was a puppy he followed me everywhere, like a shadow."

Fiona spoke up. "He follows our Tom like a shadow!"

"Mr. Fowler, Thunder and I were both orphans," Tom said. "Since then we've been adopted by

Enoch and Fiona. This is Thunder's home now."

April started to cry and Fiona went into the bedroom to get her.

"I understand how you're feeling only too well," Mr. Fowler said. "I love that dog too, and I was heartbroken when he was lost overboard in that god-awful storm. You can imagine how happy I was to hear he was rescued."

"Thunder is our hero. He saved every family on the whole island during the tidal wave," Fiona said, returning with April. "And have you heard how he and Tom brought me safely across the harbor when I was ready to give birth?" She held the baby close to Mr. Fowler. "Can you imagine what would have happened to April, without Thunder?"

Mr. Fowler looked down at the baby, who was sucking her thumb, and he sighed.

"God knew we would need him," Fiona went on. "That's why he was saved and why he came to live with us."

"Of course, we aren't really sure that Thunder and Shadow are the same dog," Enoch pointed out.

Mr. Fowler said, "What other dog would be

swimming out there that very day in that very storm?"

"Even if Thunder really *is* your dog, please don't take 'im away from us," Tom begged, his eyes brimming. He tried not to blink, but the tears slipped down his cheeks all the same.

Mr. Fowler was silent for a while. Then he said, "Let's see the dog. That's the only way we can tell once and for all if it really is my Shadow."

"Didn't you see him as you came in?" Tom asked. "He was on the porch with Amos and Bert."

"No," said Enoch. "They weren't there."

"Where *is* Thunder?" Fiona asked.

"I'll go find them," Enoch said.

At that moment Amos and Bert came through the front door with Thunder. "We just took 'im for a little walk," Amos said.

Thunder bounded in and jumped up on Tom, lapping his face. "I'll be a pickled puddick!" Tom whispered.

"Great Neptune's tongue," Enoch muttered.

Fiona gasped and seemed unable to speak.

The white zigzag lightning streak on Thunder's chest was gone!

Thunder trotted over to Mr. Fowler. He tilted his head quizzically and sniffed the man. Then, tail wagging, Thunder turned and settled at Tom's feet.

Mr. Fowler looked the dog over. "This can't be Shadow," he said. "My dog had a white flash on his chest, right about here." He traced the fur where the spot would be. When he withdrew his hand, Tom could see a black smudge on the man's finger. Mr. Fowler saw it too. He took a handkerchief from his pocket, wiped his hands, then looked up at Bert and Amos.

He knows, Tom thought. *He probably believes we've tried to trick him.*

Enoch stood up quickly. "Mr. Fowler . . . I hope you're not thinkin' . . ."

Without a word Mr. Fowler went out to the porch. Enoch started after him, but Mr. Fowler waved him off and closed the door.

Enoch turned around swiftly and glowered at Amos and Bert. "How could you do such a thing! Mr. Fowler knows that's tar on Thunder's chest! Now he thinks we're deceivin' him."

"We were only tryin' to help," Amos stammered. He took Bert by the sleeve. "Come on, son, let's go."

Bert looked over at Tom. "We was hopin' to rightify things," he said. "After all, it's our fault that Mr. Fowler showed up to claim Thunder."

Tom nodded. "I know. Thanks for tryin' anyways."

"I guess we've caused enough trouble around here," Amos said as they went out the door.

From the window Tom could see them side-step Mr. Fowler, who was sitting on the stairs.

"What is Mr. Fowler doing?" Fiona asked.

"He's just sittin' there on the steps, lookin' out at the sea," Tom answered.

Mr. Fowler was sure to take Thunder away now, especially after what Bert and Amos just did. Tom sank to his knees again and threw his arms around the dog. "Mr. Fowler is gonna take you away, Thunder. He came all this way 'cause he loves you too." Thunder whined and licked Tom's ear. "God gave you to us 'cause He knew we needed you. But now it's time for you to go." Tom's voice broke and he sobbed into Thunder's neck.

When he looked up, Mr. Fowler was standing in the doorway.

"You've been good to this dog, haven't you? I can see he loves you."

Tom nodded. "He's my best friend."

Mr. Fowler bent down and petted Thunder's head. "You're a fine dog, Thunder, and I wish you were mine. But you're not. You really are Tom's dog. You belong with him and he belongs with you. And that's the way it was meant to be."

Was Tom hearing correctly? "Do you mean—"

"He's your dog," said Mr. Fowler, patting Tom's shoulder. "Take good care of each other."

"We will, sir." Tom reached out and shook Mr. Fowler's hand over and over. "Thank you. Thank you!"

"I'll be on my way now—" the man said.

"But—" Fiona interrupted, looking perplexed.

"I'll see Mr. Fowler out," Enoch interrupted before she could say any more. He held the door open.

Mr. Fowler nodded to Fiona, shook April's little hand, and went out.

"Did you hear that, Thunder?" Tom cried. "Mr. Fowler says you're really my dog. He's not takin' you away from us." Thunder lapped Tom's face. "You clever, old slyboots."

When Enoch came back in, Fiona looked troubled. "We weren't honest, Enoch. We knew

Amos and Bert had painted Thunder's lightning streak."

"Mr. Fowler knew too," said Enoch. "The last thing he said to me was, 'Be sure to get that tar off Thunder's chest!'"

"He's a right good and kind man, that Mr. Fowler," Fiona said with a smile.

"As good a man as ever slung suspenders over his shoulders," Enoch agreed.

They went to the porch and waved as Mr. Fowler's boat backed into the harbor, then headed out to the sea.

"Well, we're a complete family now," Enoch said. "A mother"—he smiled at Fiona—"a father, a son, a daughter—"

"And a dog," Tom added.

Thunder barked and wagged his tail.

In Fiona's arms April began to cry again. "Too much excitement for our little girl." Fiona put April in Tom's arms. "Here, why don't you put her in the cradle."

Tom carried April to her room, Thunder following at his heels.

"Sh," Tom whispered as he set his sister down.

"Everything is all right now." Then he pulled the pocket watch from his pocket and tucked it under her pillow. *"Falalalee. Falalaloo."* Tom sang softly.

April sucked her finger. Her eyes gradually closed as Tom rocked the cradle. Thunder curled up on the rug next to the baby.

"Falalalee. Falalaloo."

The characters and plot in *Thunder from the Sea* are fictional. However, some of the events that take place in this book are real.

In my story Tom Campbell is an orphan from the Grenfell Mission in St. Anthony on the Northern Peninsula of Newfoundland. This internationally famous mission, hospital, and orphanage was founded in the early 1900s by Sir Wilfred Grenfell. The orphanage housed about seventy children from the Labrador and the Northern Peninsula of Newfoundland. The mission's hospital ship, *Strathcona I,* would travel to outports in Labrador and the Northern Peninsula to help the sick and poor inhabitants. In later years, my cousin, Norman Small, became captain of a newer *Strathcona.*

If ever you visit the National Cathedral in

Washington, D.C., be sure to see the stained glass window known as the "Physicians' Window" by artist Wilbur H. Burnham. In the center Christ is portrayed as "the Great Healer." On his left is Louis Pasteur and on his right is Sir Wilfred Grenfell.

Animals—dogs in particular—are instinctively aware and, at times, can warn of coming disasters like earthquakes. Perhaps they feel the ground beginning to rumble beneath their feet even before the earthquake is apparent to people.

The earthquake and tidal wave really happened in November of 1929 on the Burin Peninsula in southeastern Newfoundland. Many people were killed and houses, ships, docks, and a church were destroyed. As in the novel, some folks raced to the beach to pick up the stranded fish just before the tidal wave swept down upon them.

The trek Tom and Fiona make through the snowstorm to get to the doctor is similar to the dogsled journey my cousin, Margaret, made in the 1950s. She too traveled over a frozen bay in Newfoundland to get to the hospital to have her baby. When she returned home on the dogsled, her baby was carried in a "biscuit box" like the one that Fiona uses for April.

The tradition of mummers, or jannies, is an ancient one dating back centuries. The celebration or carnival of "mummering" was usually carried on between Christmastime and Twelfth Day. This celebration had little to do with the birth of Christ, but was a carryover from the ancient Roman celebration of the Saturnalia, which takes place at the winter solstice. In Celtic Ireland the solstice was also a time when people disguised in masks and foolish costumes went from house to house to sing and dance with weird shouts and cries and high-pitched "jannie talk." Oftentimes they enacted the traditional "Mummer's Play," which included characters such as Pickle Herring and the Fool. Horsy-hops, also known as Hobby Horse, was a weird figure bearing the head of a horse with a mouth that clanked open, displaying iron teeth. Mummering was often boisterous and rowdy and was banned in Newfoundland in 1892 as a "public nuisance." People who continue with this tradition often ask to be invited into the house they are visiting by inquiring, "Good mummers allowed?" Mummers or jannies usually speak with inhaled breath and high-pitched voices and run all their words together to keep their disguises.

Cheek music, also called chin music or mouth music, is made by singing nonsensical syllables that rhyme and have rhythm. You probably have sung cheek music many times without knowing it. "Bippity boppity boo" from Disney's *Cinderella* is a good example of cheek music. Another is the Irish lullabye, "Toora loora loora." And of course Mary Poppins's "Supercalafragalisticexpialidocious!"

The colorful language, superstitions, and folklore in this story have been collected from all over Newfoundland. The pronunciation of certain words and the meanings of some lore vary from one harbor or village to another. I've gathered them together and given them to my characters who dwell on the imaginary island of Back o' the Moon and in the fictional outport of Chance-Along.

A dog who was rescued from an Atlantic gale was the inspiration for Thunder. Several years ago I read the tale of a beautiful Newfoundland dog named Prince, who disappeared overboard from a fishing boat in a wild Atlantic storm in 1897. The owners gave him up for lost, but amazingly the dog survived and was rescued by a Gloucester, Massachusetts, vessel and taken back to Gloucester, where the schooner that saved him became his home. He sailed many voyages on that ship and good fishing was always attributed to Prince. However, years later, when the skipper was about to take another voyage, the dog refused to go. He strained to get away and barked loudly, as if in protest. The crew went without him—and never returned. Was Prince giving a warning to the Gloucester schooner and its crew?

As you can see, bits and pieces of the past—things I've read or learned or shared—became borrowed threads that have been woven into this new story, *Thunder from the Sea*. I hope you enjoyed reading it as much as I enjoyed writing it.

Read on for a sneak peek at Joan Hiatt Harlow's

Midnight Rider

Hot wind blew through the open casement window. Hannah tossed on the bed, her legs tangling in the quilt. "Mama," she whispered. Was that her voice—hoarse and painful? Where was Mama? She wanted so much to curl up in her mother's lap.

"Your mother is gone," a voice said. "Don't you remember?"

Hannah opened her eyes. Aunt Phoebe was standing over her, her black hair pulled into a bun that made her dark eyes seem cold and sharp.

Then Hannah remembered.

Her mother had died of the smallpox. Mama was gone—like Papa. They were both gone forever.

Hannah pulled away the sleeve of her shift. Through the tears that blurred her vision she saw that her arm was covered with angry pustules. Sores oozed and burned with each movement of her body. She had the pox too! She closed her eyes as Phoebe pressed a cold, wet cloth to her face. "Thank you, Aunt Phoebe." She spoke painfully. The sores from the smallpox crusted on her throat.

Hannah turned her face to the window to see the green pasture rolling across the Salem hillside. Her black gelding, Promise, was grazing near the old elm tree. Promise had been left outside all summer. Since Aunt Phoebe was afraid of horses, there was no one to put him in the barn. Hannah wondered if she would ever ride again with the wind in her hair and Promise beneath her.

With her fever, headache, and terrible sores, days and nights intermingled. There were fleeting visions of Aunt Phoebe standing over the bed.

One morning when Aunt Phoebe brought Hannah her usual tea and slice of molasses bread, she said, "You've passed the crisis. You'll recover, Hannah." Aunt Phoebe then bathed her with herbs, shaking her head over the number of scabs on Hannah's body. "At least your face has been spared. Only this one scab embedded on your cheek will leave a scar. It will serve as a reminder that outward beauty is only vanity," she muttered.

When Phoebe left the room, Hannah turned to the open window. Promise must be out there waiting for her. She could hear a lark singing from the common pasture, and she could see Farmer Anderson's cows. But Promise was not in his customary grazing place.

Hannah threw back the quilt and climbed out of bed to get a better look. Her legs felt as weak as bent reeds as she made her way unsteadily to the casement window. Pushing the window open wide, she thrust her head outside. "Promise!" Usually, at the sound of her voice, Promise would stop grazing, prick up his ears, and look around eagerly to see where Hannah might be.

Hannah scanned the entire pasture. Promise was gone!

"Aunt Phoebe!" Hannah called. "Where is Promise?"

Aunt Phoebe, her hands folded in front of her, was standing in the doorway, her face without expression. "I sold the horse."

"No! You didn't! Promise is my horse—Papa's gift to me." Hannah's knees buckled and she fell to the floor. Through a sea of tears she looked up at her aunt, who now towered above her. "Please, Aunt Phoebe," she sobbed. "Please tell me you didn't sell my horse."

The woman took hold of Hannah's arm and pulled her to her feet. "Get back to bed," she said.

"No!" Hannah pulled away. "Tell me what you've done!"

Aunt Phoebe took a deep breath. "I cannot afford to keep a horse. Farmer Anderson has helped me take care of Promise since you and your mother got sick, but I cannot ask him to continue feeding that animal for you. In a few months it will be winter. Who will pay for oats or hay?" She smoothed her apron. "It costs enough for both of *us* to eat, without feeding a horse as well."

"But Promise helped with plowing and the carriage..." Hannah stopped. She knew only too well from the way Aunt Phoebe's eyes narrowed and her lips tightened into a thin line that the matter was settled.

Aunt Phoebe continued. "I've taken care of you

and your mother until my back is broken. The least you can do is be grateful and not complain about the decisions I make." She headed for the doorway.

Hannah climbed into the bed and closed her eyes. Tears squeezed out from under her lashes, stinging the still-red pockmark on her face.

"Dear Lord," she prayed. "Please help me to be grateful. Please help me to be strong. And please, please bring Promise back to me."

a fter she recovered, Hannah visited her mother's grave nearly every day. It had been almost two months now since that dreadful day in May when her mother died. The morning fog was lifting as Hannah brushed her hands across the granite headstone with its ugly skull. Once again she read the engraved words:

Here lieth Luvena Andrews, wife and mother,
who awaiteth the resurrection trumpet
                    Born 1740   Died 1774

Hannah knew about the resurrection, for Mama, who came from a Puritan background, had diligently read the Scriptures with her. The minister, Thomas Barnard, reminded Hannah that Elijah, Elisha, and Jesus raised people from the dead and brought them back to their families. Mr. Barnard said that God would raise her mother, too, but not until the resurrection trumpet sounded on the "last day" spoken of in the Bible. It seemed like a long time to wait.

A rooster crowed in the distance and a horse neighed. Hannah saw a boy galloping across the meadow. Until recently the meadow had been a muddy marshland due to the heavy spring rains. But the hot July sun had dried the soil, and today, as the sun broke through, the damp marsh was transformed into an emerald sea of grass where sparkling wildflowers became rubies and topaz. On a day as beautiful as this, Hannah longed to race across the fields with Promise. But Promise was gone.

Now Hannah rejoiced at the sight of the boy riding bareback through the meadow, his sun-streaked brown hair blowing in the breeze. That horse he was riding looked so much like Promise! She scurried to the stone wall that marked the common pasture and the town graveyard, then ran alongside it, her attention on the ebony horse.

Hannah scrambled over the wall and onto the field, waving her hands and calling, "Promise! Promise!"

The horse stopped suddenly, then turned, his ears twitching. Startled, the boy almost slipped off, and he yanked the reins angrily. The horse reared and headed in Hannah's direction. "Stop! Stop, Midnight!" the boy yelled, trying to turn the horse back. But the animal continued to make his way to Hannah.

"How dare you frighten my horse!" the boy yelled as he came closer. "Don't you have a brain? I could have been killed!"

"Promise is *my* horse," Hannah retorted as she ran and threw her arms around Promise's neck. "Nothing could keep him away from me." Hannah stroked the horse's shining mane. "I have missed you, my darling boy."

"He's not yours," the rider said. "My father bought him for me."

Hannah drew herself up tall to look up at the stranger. "My father gave *me* this horse, and his name is Promise. He knows my voice. That's why he stopped when I called him."

"Ah, perhaps that's why the horse has been so skittish. He misses you. He hasn't been eating much either." The boy slid off the horse. "We bought this gelding from that Andrews lady. She said the horse was hers."

"That Andrews lady is my aunt Phoebe," said Hannah. "My name is Hannah Andrews."

"I'm Will Samson. We moved into the farm over near the willows."

So this was why Aunt Phoebe had explicitly told her not to speak with the new family that moved into that farm, Hannah realized angrily. Aunt Phoebe didn't want her to know that Promise was somewhere in Salem.

"We paid good and true money for this horse. So he's mine now."

"How much did you pay?" Hannah was curious.

"Eighty pounds sterling." Will cocked his head. "Didn't your aunt tell you?"

"No." Hannah stroked Promise, who nuzzled her arm.

"If this horse is yours, then the money is yours."

"Aunt Phoebe will keep the money, I'm sure."

"Where did you ever get a name like Promise?"

"Papa brought him to me when I was ten. Papa said, 'I promised you a horse of your own.' Right then and there, I named him Promise." Tears welled in Hannah's eyes, and she turned away.

"Where's your papa now?"

"He died two years ago." Hannah paused, recalling mornings riding behind her father along an Indian trace by the Merrimack River in Chelmsford. They'd stop to pick daisies for Mama while Promise grazed in the meadow. "We came to live in Salem after he died. Now my mother is dead too."

"My pa said that lots of families around here were struck with the pox. Is that what happened to you and your ma?" His gaze fixed on her cheek.

Hannah flushed and pulled a strand of hair over the pockmark. "Yes. Mama was the first to fall ill. Then I got it and almost died too. Sometimes I wish I had." She nodded toward the burial ground. "Mama's grave is over there."

"I'm right sad to hear that," he said. "You must be greatly sorrowed."

Hannah nodded, but then smiled. "To see Promise again is a joyful thing."

Will stroked the neck of the horse. "He's a beauty."

The horse seemed to sense that they were talking about him and tossed his head. Hannah stroked his black neck again. "Aunt Phoebe told me not to speak with your family nor trespass on your land."

"She probably doesn't want you to know where the horse is, or how much we paid for him. She's a fox when it comes to money." Will shook his head. "And she's not a pleasant woman—in fact, if she'd been living here in Salem a hundred years ago, she'd have burned as a witch." His lips twitched into a grin.

Hannah stifled a laugh, then said solemnly, "Aunt Phoebe was good to us when we were sick. She tells me often how"—Hannah wrinkled up her nose and mimicked her aunt's self-righteous speech—"'I've given up everything to help you and your mother! My whole life has changed. And not for the better, I might add.'"

"You sound just like her!" Will said with a laugh. "But why are you here talking to me and disobeying your aunt's wishes? If she finds out, she'll give you a whipping."

"When she sold Promise, she hurt me more than any whipping." Hannah put her arms around the horse's neck. "Will, perhaps you should keep his name Promise. He's not used to Midnight."

"I'll do some thinking on it," Will agreed.

"I hope you're good to him." Promise nuzzled his soft nose into Hannah's face and nickered softly.

"Of course I'm good to him." Will smiled. "Would you like a ride?"

"Oh, indeed I would!" Hannah exclaimed.

Will held his hands together for Hannah to mount, which she did in a flash, pulling her skirt above her knees.

Will handed her the reins and was about to climb on the horse behind her, but Hannah clicked her heels into the horse's flank and yelled, "Giddap, Promise!"

As the horse bounded away, Hannah waved at Will, who was left behind, his hands on his hips. She and Promise galloped across the meadow, around a stand of white birches, and to the top of a small hill from where she could see the sapphire Atlantic Ocean sparkling in the distance. Down the hill they flew, into the north fields, where they came across a rapid brook. Promise slowed momentarily to keep his footing, then splashed through the water. Hannah laughed as the cold water splattered on her bare legs. They darted back across the meadow to the stone wall where Will was waiting.

Before Will could speak, Hannah pulled the reins and slid off the horse. "Thank you for letting me ride my horse again."

Will's mouth opened and shut in astonishment. "You ride like a wild thing!" he finally said. Promise nudged Hannah with his nose, as if inviting her to ride again. "He likes you," Will said.

Hannah stroked the horse's neck. "He *loves* me."

"Would you like to ride another day?"

"Oh, yes!" Hannah nodded eagerly. "I visit my mother's grave every morning."

Hannah's gloom diminished over the next few weeks, and sometimes she even sang as she helped Aunt Phoebe in the gardens and around the house. Hannah could sense her aunt watching her closely.

Almost every day she secretly met Will at the graveyard wall and rode Promise.

One late July morning they sat on the stone wall and talked. "I'm going to ride into Boston one day soon," Will told Hannah.

"Why?"

"I want to help the cause of freedom in Boston Town. Haven't you heard about all that's happening there? England has been unfairly sticking taxes and laws on Americans."

"Everyone's heard how Bostonians masqueraded as Mohawk Indians and dumped all the tea into the harbor rather than be taxed on it," Hannah broke in.

"It's not that Americans won't pay taxes," Will explained. "It's that we don't get representation. Parliament over there in London doesn't give an owl's hoot about us. They've left us alone all these years, and they've suddenly realized that *we're* thriving and *they're* in debt. Now they want our money—and we don't get a say about anything!" Will's voice rose. "They're even forcing Bostonians to quarter redcoat soldiers in their homes—to feed them and give them beds."

"It sounds dreadful in Boston," Hannah said.

"I want to help the Whigs work toward freedom from England."

"We have Whigs here in Salem, don't we?"

"Indeed we do. My father's a Whig. Whigs are trying to work peacefully with England for our rights," Will told her. "But lately most want freedom from England."

Hannah had heard Aunt Phoebe speak with loathing of Whigs and Patriots. She spoke of herself as a Loyalist. "What do Loyalists want?" Hannah asked.

"Loyalists want America to stay loyal to King George and England," Will explained. "They're also called Tories."

"Aunt Phoebe is a Loyalist—a Tory," Hannah said.

"I heard tell that General Gage is heading back to Boston." Will went on. "He's the one who closed off Boston Harbor so no ships or supplies can get into that town. That's why Salem's the main port for shipping now. But people say he's in danger living around these parts, so he's moving back to Boston to keep order there. He's not well liked, no matter where he goes."

"I would think he'd be in more danger in Boston," Hannah said. "Especially after the Boston Massacre."

"Right. Can you believe British soldiers killed five Bostonians in that riot? One of them, Christopher Seider, was just a boy. Bostonians have never forgotten it."

"I wouldn't want to go to Boston if I were you, Will. Besides," Hannah added hesitantly, "I'd miss you."

Will's face flushed, and he looked down. "Oh, you'd miss the horse, not me."

Aunt Phoebe suddenly came up behind them. "So this is what you've been up to, you ungrateful child! I saw you astride that horse with your skirt up and bare legs showing!" She pointed a long finger at Hannah. "I'm not putting up with this!"